Nelly the MONSTeR Sitter

Nelly the MONSTER Sitter

Grerks, Squurms & Water Greeps

KES GRAY

Illustrated by Stephen Hanson

razOr
bill

To the Tillinghasts at number two

RAZORBILL
Published by the Penguin Group
Penguin Young Readers Group
345 Hudson Street, New York, New York 10014, U.S.A.
Penguin Group (USA) Inc., 375 Hudson Street, New York, New York 10014, U.S.A.
Penguin Group (Canada), 90 Eglinton Avenue East, Suite 700, Toronto, Ontario,
Canada M4P 2Y3 (a division of Pearson Penguin Canada Inc.)
Penguin Books Ltd, 80 Strand, London WC2R 0RL, England
Penguin Ireland, 25 St Stephen's Green, Dublin 2, Ireland
(a division of Penguin Books Ltd)
Penguin Group (Australia), 250 Camberwell Road, Camberwell,
Victoria 3124, Australia (a division of Pearson Australia Group Pty Ltd)
Penguin Books India Pvt Ltd, 11 Community Centre,
Panchsheel Park, New Delhi – 110 017, India
Penguin Group (NZ), 67 Apollo Drive, Mairangi Bay, Auckland 1311,
New Zealand (a division of Pearson New Zealand Ltd)
Penguin Books (South Africa) (Pty) Ltd, 24 Sturdee Avenue,
Rosebank, Johannesburg 2196, South Africa

Penguin Books Ltd, Registered Offices: 80 Strand, London WC2R 0RL, England

First published in Great Britain in 2004 by Hodder Children's Books

10 9 8 7 6 5 4 3 2 1

Copyright 2009 © Kes Gray
All rights reserved

Library of Congress Cataloging-in-Publication Data is available

Razorbill ISBN 978-1-59514-259-7

Printed in the United States of America

NELLY THE MONSTER SITTER

"If monsters are real, how come I've never seen one?" said Nelly.

"Because they never go out," said her dad.

"Why don't monsters ever go out?" said Nelly.

"Because they can never get a baby sitter," said her dad.

Nelly thought about it. Her mom and dad never went out unless they could get a baby sitter. Why should monsters be any different?

"Then I will become Nelly the Monster Sitter!" smiled Nelly.

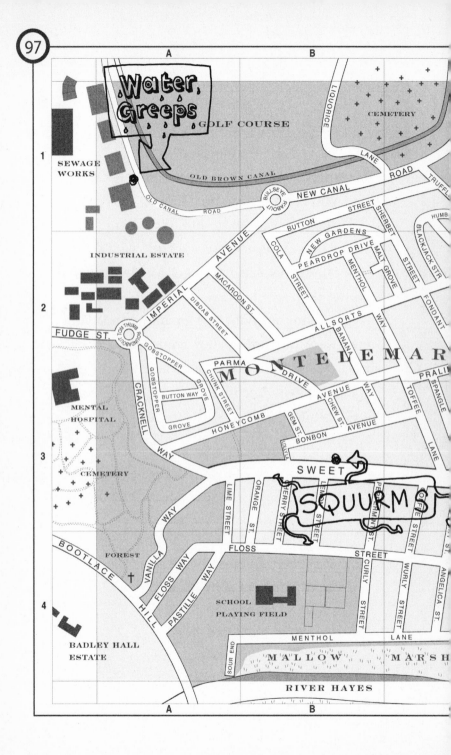

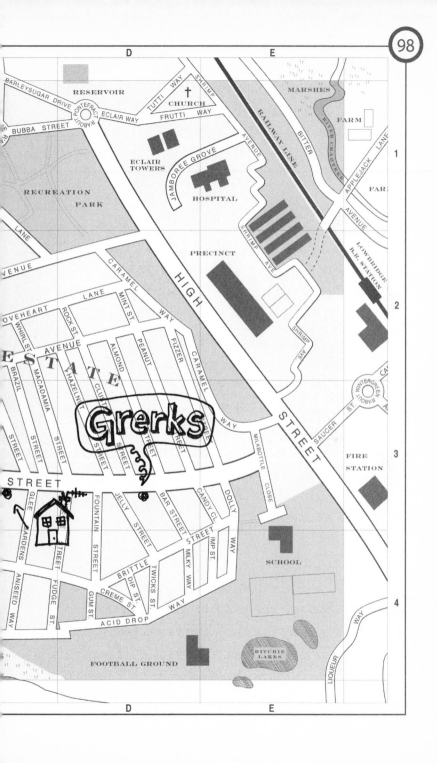

1

There were four drawers in Petronella Morton's bedside cabinet. Three were as dull as school, one was extra special with a secret hidden inside. Nelly, as she much preferred to be called, knelt down excitedly in front of drawer number four and slowly eased it open.

Her eyes dropped inside and fell upon the crisp clean folds of a freshly ironed pair of blue and pink stripy pajamas. She lifted the pajamas up slightly, counted four jumpers down and then slipped her fingers into the fold beneath. A spark ignited in both her eyes as her fingers withdrew the secret from its hiding place. She lay it on her lap, paused for a moment and then stroked it lovingly with the tips of her fingers.

It was a lime green hot-water bottle. *Made in Taiwan. Do not overfill.*

Nelly cradled it in her lap for a moment and then opened the flat end of the water bottle like a pitta bread. Unbeknown to her family, she had changed the use of the water bottle entirely by slicing open the widest end with a craft knife, creating a secret cavity inside.

She slipped her fingers into the cavity and pulled out her pride and joy. It was a notebook, spiral bound. The plain red cover had been transformed by the addition of a large handwritten title rendered with silver and gold glitter pens. The title of the book read: *Nelly the Monster Sitter's Secret Monster Sitting Notebook* (in gold) – *KEEP OUT OR ELSE* (double underlined in silver, three exclamation marks– !!!).

Nelly's secret monster-sitting notebook was for Nelly's eyes only. Not that Nelly was a secretive girl. Indeed she shared nearly all of her innermost thoughts with her family (not including her sister Astilbe). She had simply learned that some of the things that she saw when she went monster sitting were best kept to herself. You know – gunky, slimy, spiky stuff that other people can find scary or hair raising.

Monster sitting was Nelly's special thing. None of her friends would ever dare baby sit for a family of monsters, or even knock on a monster's front door. Just about everyone Nelly knew, including her twin sister Asti (as she much preferred to be called), thought that monsters were freaks to be avoided rather than neighbors to be welcomed. But then Nelly wasn't like most other children. Or people, for that matter.

She had a heart the size of an air balloon and nerves as steady as an oil rig.

Thankfully for Nelly, her mom and dad were generous spirited too. From day one, they had been totally fine with Nelly's idea of helping monsters to get out of the house a little bit more. Nelly's dad was of the mind that baby sitting for

monsters would be "educational." Nelly's mom
was hoping it might help Nelly with her table
manners. For sure, Nelly was lucky to have parents
like Clifford and Yvonne Morton.

She opened her secret notebook and flicked
randomly past some pages headed in her own
handwriting HOJPOGS, WIZZILS, and GLOO-
BLES. She found the next empty page and pulled
the lid off a gel pen with her teeth. At the top of
the page, in her best purple, she wrote the heading "Grerks's" and then followed it with three
dots.

Three dots meant "*more info later.*"

Nelly was pencilled into her diary to monster
sit later that evening. She had never monster
sat a Grerk before and it wouldn't be until she
returned home later that evening that she would
be able to complete her notes.

She knew what Grerks sounded like over
the telephone, in fact she had mistaken their
squeaking squawks for a Squiddl. But as for ap-
pearances? Were they scaly, were they spiky or

slimy or furry? For Nelly, half the fun was guessing, the other half was finding out.

The Grerks from number 55 had asked Nelly if she could monster sit from six until eight that evening. It was twenty to six already, and Nelly hadn't even sat down for her afternoon snack.

She slipped her secret notebook back into its water bottle and placed it carefully back into the drawer. She was pushing the drawer shut, when the handle on her bedroom door began to twist, rattle and shake.

"Why have you locked it?" shouted her sister from the other side of Nelly's bedroom door.

"So Barbies can't get in," shouted Nelly, who most days of the week didn't get along with her sister much, and the other days of the week didn't get along with her at all.

"Let me in now or I'll tell Mom!" shouted Asti.

Nelly ignored her sister's protests and opened the door of her wardrobe instead. She took out her favorite, coolest sweatshirt and laid it on the bed. It was purple with an orange trim and it had the word *sardine* printed across the chest in big swirly silver letters. No one, including Nelly, understood why the word sardine had been printed on the sweatshirt. But that was precisely why Nelly liked it. Because it was different.

As she tied back her licorice black hair with a yellow scrunchy, the bedroom door handle rattled furiously again.

"Let me IN!" squawked Asti.

Nelly smiled, opened the door and barged past her sister.

"Freak lover," said Asti.

"Bog tentacle," said Nelly.

Asti placed her hands on her hips and glared at the back of Nelly's purple sweatshirt as it breezed past her in the direction of the stairs. She wasn't as quick thinking as Nelly and needed time to upgrade her next insult. The words *Smelly*, *Freako* and *Weirdo* flew around in her brain, but by the time she had hit upon "Freak lover," Nelly had disappeared from view.

As usual Nelly was ten steps ahead of her sister. She bounced down the stairs and wheeled towards the kitchen in the faint hope that tea might be ready and waiting for her on the table. But as usual, a bottle of tomato sauce was the only thing on hand.

Mealtime had never been a simple affair in Nelly's house. Her mom was a vegetarian, her dad ate like a lion, her sister was a fuss-pot and Nelly didn't like carrots. Actually, she secretly didn't *mind* carrots, but seeing as everyone else in her family was so picky about what they ate, she had decided to have a mealtime no-no of her own.

Nelly walked into the kitchen and found her mom looking perplexed. She was staring at the kitchen counter trying to work out what she could cook for everyone that would involve the minimom amount of effort and the least amount of cleaning up.

"Mom," said Nelly, "is my snack ready, 'cos I'm monster sitting at six and I need to leave in ten minutes."

Nelly's mom stared blankly at the ingredients in front of her, replacing the chicken nuggets with fish sticks and then swapping a box of maca-roni cheese for three large sticks of celery and an avocado. "I really wish you liked carrots, Nelly, it

Nelly's mom stared blankly at the ingredients in front of her.

would make life so much easier," said her mom, trying to shift the blame on to Nelly's shoulders.

"Why don't we get take-out?" suggested Nelly, sensing an opportunity to avoid her mom's cooking.

Nelly's mom threw her arms up into the air. "Brilliant idea!" she said, sweeping the avocado and celery back into the vegetable rack and tossing an assortment of tins back into the cabinet. "A pizza it is!"

"Can we order it for eight o'clock?" asked Nelly. "I'll be back just after."

"Brilliant, brilliant!" said Nelly's mom, bending the herring back into an overly full compartment of the freezer. "I'll go and put my feet up for a couple of hours. I could do with a break. I wonder what's on TV?"

"The usual Saturday night garbage," said Nelly's dad, limping into the kitchen from the garden. "It's always bad TV on a Saturday."

"Why are you sucking your thumb, Dad?" asked Nelly.

"Snowball," winced her dad.

"You've been poking your fingers through the rabbit cage again, haven't you?" said her mom. "You know Snowball only likes Nelly."

It was true. The Morton family rabbit was a one-person rabbit. As white as snow and as fluffy as thistledown. He lived in a hutch on the patio, making regular day trips to the lawn courtesy of a portable rabbit run. He looked as cutesy wutesy as a bunnykins could look, but lurking beneath that little twitchy nose and those soft whiskers was a killerkins, two needle sharp teeth with enough strength to crunch through a steel carrot and meet in the middle. Nelly had never been sure why Snowball had singled her out as his one true friend in the world, but hey, if it made Asti jealous it had to be a good thing.

Nelly's dad threw a pitiful glance at his wife and then limped to the kitchen sink. (Nelly's dad always limped when he was looking for sympathy.)

"Why are you limping again?" asked Nelly's

mom. "Next you'll be telling me the rabbit tripped you up, as well!"

"Maybe Snowball picked Dad up, swung him around his head and body slammed him onto the patio!" laughed Nelly.

Nelly's dad sighed. If he was looking for sympathy then he was most certainly in the wrong room at the wrong time with the wrong people.

Things tipped slightly more in his favor with the arrival of Asti.

"Ooh poor Dad!" she cooed, seeing that her father was in mild distress and seizing the opportunity to gain some major brownie points. Nelly groaned inwardly as her sister ran across the kitchen and threw her arms around her dad's waist.

"Ooh that's awful, does it hurt?" she gushed. "How did it happen?"

"Snowball," gasped her dad bravely.

"I hate that rabbit," snapped Asti angrily, "we should get rid of him before someone gets killed."

"Ooh that's awful, does it hurt?"

Nelly looked at her mom, Nelly's mom looked at Nelly's dad. Everyone looked at Asti. For a girl with very little imagination she had certainly surpassed herself this time. Asti tried to backtrack.

"OK, not *killed* exactly, but what if Snowball bit someone and they got Rabbit-titis or something? What then?"

No one was convinced.

"Oh I give up!" sighed Asti, glaring at her dad and then flouncing back upstairs to put on some more cherry lip-gloss. "It's only a nip and anyway you should be on my side because *I* was on *yours.*"

Nelly looked at her watch and sidled towards the front door.

"I'll be back just after eight," she said, writing the Grerks's telephone number and house number on a pink Post-it note and sticking it on the hall mirror by the front door.

"Can I have extra cheese with chillies please," requested Nelly, "and some garlic bread to ward away evil Astis!"

"Stop winding your sister up," growled her mom. "And don't forget to leave the Grerks's telephone num—"

"I've stuck it in the usual place," said Nelly, grabbing her coat from its coat hook and opening the front door.

"I hope some disgusting twelve-headed swamp monster eats you," cackled Asti from the top of the stairs.

"They always lose their appetite once I've told them about you," smiled Nelly.

Asti wavered at the top of the stairs, stung by another quick-fire Nellyism. But before she had time to even raise her foot to stamp it, Nelly had skipped triumphantly into the front garden and closed the door.

"Slime lover!" shouted Asti, rather late, even by her standards.

2

For Nelly Morton, monster sitting was a chance to be like her sweatshirt. Different. Especially different from her sister, Asti. Life can be so *samey* when you're a twin. Everyone expects you to be one half of the same person, to wear the same clothes, to do the same things, to feel the same way. Everyone jumps to the same samey conclusions about you both and yet Nelly wasn't like Asti at all. OK, she and Asti were similarish to look at, but in every other way they were as different as no and yes.

Nelly wasn't afraid of monsters. Asti was. Nelly thought monsters were lovely. Asti didn't. Nelly didn't mind shaking a seven fingered paw. Asti did. Nelly was happy to play leapfrog with a four-foot tall amphibious creature with long dangly tentacles and suckers on its forehead. Asti wasn't. Being a monster sitter had given Nelly the chance to prove it. Monsters were Nelly's own special territory. Only six months after placing her first monster-sitting advertisement in the local paper, Sweet Street and the whole of the Montelimar Estate had become Nelly's special monster-sitting patch.

She never monster sat for money, she did it mostly to be helpful but also for the excitement. For on each occasion she had monster sat, whether she had turned left out of the gate or right out of the gate, a monster adventure had loomed. She was sure that this evening would be no different.

The street that Nelly lived on was a very long street, busyish with traffic during the early and late parts of the day but quieter during the afternoon hours. Nelly's house was located somewhere roughly in the middle. "Roughly" is probably the wrong word to use because there was nothing rough about Sweet Street at all. On weekends especially, when people swapped their cars for lawn mowers, it was really a very pleasant street to live on. Sweet Street was a very respectable street. A very safe street. It was neat and tidy in the garden department and crowned on either side with pollarded lime trees.

The lime trees and that strange "p word" had become a huge talking point in the street that winter. One crisp February day Nelly had watched a tree surgeon in a fluorescent orange jacket lop all the branches off the limes with a chain saw. Apparently that's what "pollarding" means, chopping all the branches off right down to the trunk. Even now, late into spring, as Nelly walked in the direction of number 55 she was still unsure of the results. Basically the trees didn't look like trees anymore. Without their branches the spindly growth that had sprouted from the stumps on top made them look like giant shaving brushes. She had thought of protesting to Greenpeace about it but had decided they were probably too busy saving whales.

Twelve shaving brushes further down the street, Nelly began to take notice of the house numbers that were approaching. Number 55 was an odd number. That meant that on this particular monster visit, there would be no need for her to cross the road.

She glanced low along the garden walls of the houses that she was nearing. The first set of polished brass letters read number 73. She guessed there were about ten more houses to go.

"Scaly, four ears and two heads. I bet that's what a Grerk looks like... or maybe three heads," she mused.

For Nelly, one of the best parts about monster sitting was guessing what a monster family would look like before she actually met them.

Her eyes darted across the tops of a line of privet hedging and then glanced diagonally across, trying to glean a clue from the color of the front door.

63... 61... 59... 57... 55.

"Four eyes," smiled Nelly to herself. "A purple front door always means four eyes!"

She paused at the front gate, adjusted her scrunchy and then ironed her sweatshirt with the palms of her hand. First impressions were very important to Nelly.

So was being on time. She looked at her watch. It was 5:59 and forty-seven seconds. She composed herself for thirteen seconds, walked jauntily down the path to the purple front door and pressed the custard-yellow door bell hard with her finger. The doorbell gurgled loudly.

"Definitely four eyes," she smiled to herself. "Or I'm a Grimp's hairdo!"

3

The moment her finger released the door bell a fearsome wolfish growl erupted in the hallway on the other side of the door. Nelly stared at the purple high-gloss door and stood her ground. Squeaks and squawks were approaching now.

The low rasping sound of a heavy bolt sliding back was quickly followed by the rattle of a chain being released from its keep. Nelly stood straight backed as the door of number 55 opened slowly with a creak.

Nelly's eyes sky-scrapered to the top of the door. A pink onion-sized eye was staring inquisitively down at her. Nelly's eyes lowered and were met by a second eye. She dropped her sights again and began counting under her breath. One, two, three, four pink eyes were socketed

The Grerks at Number 55

like traffic lights inside a huge cabbage-green head that ballooned from a starched white shirt collar and tie, like a huge bubble gum bubble.

Nelly held her nerve as a pair of thin amphibious lips broke into a broad welcoming smile.

"Are you Nelly the Monster Sitter?" asked the goofy toothed mouth, with a shrill squeaking squawk.

"That's me!" gasped Nelly, jumping backwards down the path as a second head with two orange dangly tongues suddenly appeared from the bottom of the door and lunged in the direction of her knees. "You must be the Grerks!"

A squeaking squawking commotion erupted from behind the door as the four eyes at the top tried to keep track of the two tongues at the bottom. Nelly kept her distance and watched curiously as first the door closed then reopened, then closed again. When it reopened for the third time it swung back all the way.

Two large, green, amphibious monsters were

now standing in the hallway. One of them was cradling a smaller and considerably wriggly monster in its arms.

"We're so sorry about that, Nelly," said the Grerk that still had all three of its tentacles dangling free. "We hope he didn't frighten you. He gets so excited when he sees strangers. Please, let me introduce ourselves. My name is Scroot, this is my wife Pummice and this is our beautiful little baby, Glug."

Nelly stepped forward and held out her hand. "I'm very pleased to meet you," she said, interpreting ten twinkling eyes and two dangling tongues as an invitation to enter the house.

Nelly followed the green scaly tips of the Grerks's tails as they snaked along the hallway past a pasting table piled high with rolls of purple hairy wallpaper. It was the strangest hallway she had ever seen. The walls were dark and hairy but the floorboards were light and bare. The skirting boards that ran the length of the hall were fluorescent pink and the ceiling was a swirling

*"My name is Scroot, this is my wife Pummice and
this is our beautiful little baby, Glug."*

hotchpotch of yellows, greens and browns.

"Watch the bucket!" squawked Pummice, leading Nelly into the house. "We're in the middle of re-decorating!"

Nelly looked down at a large turquoise bucket full to the brim with a pea-green slop.

"Sorry about the mess," squeaked Scroot.

"No need to apologize," said Nelly, skirting her way around the bucket, "I'm thinking of redecorating my bedroom, too!"

"Well, if you need any wallpaper we've got lots of rolls left over!" laughed Scroot.

"I don't think I'm strong enough to hang wallpaper *that* heavy," said Nelly, suspecting that one roll alone probably weighed as much as a shaggy dog.

"Quick drying Monsta-Paste, that's all you need," squeaked Pummice, pointing to the bucket.

"And a big brush!" squawked Scroot.

Nelly smiled and followed the Grerks into the living room. There she found another room of the house in total disarray. There were cans of lemon and black spotted paint piled up by the window, pink and brown gooey swatches smeared onto the bare walls and a large strip of hairy wallpaper slapped slapdash to the wall behind the sofa. At least Nelly assumed it was a sofa. It was hard to tell because all the furniture in the room was wrapped up in silver foil.

"It protects the fabric," said Pummice, pre-empting Nelly's question.

Nelly sat down with a soft aluminium crunch and stared at the yet to be decorated walls.

"We can't decide whether to go hairy or slimy in here," said Scroot. "We've been decorating for days and we need a break! We're so pleased you could come over, Nelly, and look after our lovely little baby for us."

"My pleasure!" said Nelly, easing back on to her sofa and smiling politely across the room at her boggle-eyed hosts.

"Isn't he ugliful!" squeaked Pummice, kissing Glug tenderly on the nose with her purple rosebud lips.

Scroot joined his wife proudly on the sofa, placing two tentacles around her shoulder and the other along the back of the sofa.

Nelly smiled politely and then took a moment to weigh up the features of the three monsters that were sitting before her. There was something that she couldn't quite work out.

Glug looked so different from Pummice and Scroot! For one thing he had two eyes instead of four. He had two tongues instead of one, and six legs instead of two. He sat low and squat like a spider-legged pig, and he had five tails that wouldn't stop wagging. Even if you put his wriggliness down to the exuberance of youth and even if you completely discounted the blue satin bow that was fixed to the top of his head, the dissimilarity between Glug and his parents was quite striking.

Nelly watched as Pummice lowered Glug gently down on the floor and then braced herself as his two orange tongues came slobbering and slavering her way.

"He likes you!" squealed Pummice. "Look, I've never seen his tails wag so fast!"

Nelly slid off the armchair on to her knees and welcomed Glug with open arms.

He was big for a baby, about the size of a goat. And boy could he lick. Nelly closed her eyes and pursed her lips. Whichever way she turned, a tongue was waiting to greet her.

"If you don t mind me saying," she gasped between slurps, "he doesn't look very much like you!"

Pummice and Scroot turned to each other. Their pink onion eyes blinked softly at one another and then one by one their thin reptilian lips cracked open with uncontrollable laughter.

"Of course he doesn't look like us, Nelly! He's a gog! Glug isn't a Grerk, he's a gog! Don't you have gogs at home, Nelly?"

Nelly grimaced as Glug used his tongue like a pasting brush to slap saliva across her ear and then giggled as she realized her mistake.

"We have *dogs* not *gogs!*" blurted Nelly, deciding that she'd had quite enough Glug slobber for one visit. Fending him off with one arm, she eased herself back on to the silver foil and wiped her face with her sleeve.

Sensing that the fuss was over, Glug turned his attentions elsewhere, scurrying across the floor, jumping back into Pummice's lap and flipping over expectantly on to his back.

"He loves having his tum tickled," said Pummice, obliging with all three tentacles.

Nelly smiled uncertainly. She had never baby sat a monster *pet* before.

"He's no ordinary gog, either, Nelly," boasted Scroot. "Glug is a Pedigree Best of Breed Golden Revolver. He's been Supreme Ugly Champion at Grunts for the last three years running!"

"And tomorrow you're going to win again, aren't you, Ugliful?" said Pummice, giving his hairy tum an extra scratch. "We're going to buy our Gluggy Wuggy a beautiful new bow and a sparkling new

collar for tomorrow's show, aren't we?"

Nelly didn't know what to say. She knew that surprises always lurked behind a monster's front door, but she had never given a moments thought to gog sitting. She smiled warily as Pummice lifted Glug down on to the floor, stood up and brushed herself down.

"We really should be off, Nelly, before the late-night shopping ends. We have to buy some more pedigree gog food too. Would it be all right if we leave you a couple of instructions before we go?"

Nelly stood up dutifully and followed Pummice and Scroot into the kitchen. "Of course you can," she said, scanning the spotlessly clean surfaces of the pink and lime-green stripy kitchen units.

Scroot opened a kitchen cupboard door, reached up high with a tentacle and slapped some suckers around a large can of alligator chunks.

"It's very important that you give Glug his dinner at seven o'clock. Champion show gogs have a very carefully controlled dietary routine. Remember Nelly, seven o'clock. No later, no sooner."

Nelly turned and looked at Glug, who was panting excitedly by her feet.

"I promise I'll remember," smiled Nelly. "Can you leave me out a can opener?"

Pummice plunged her tentacles into a kitchen drawer and placed the can opener on top of the can of alligator chunks, triggering all five of Glug's tails to wag madly.

"Later, Glug, later," smiled Nelly, guessing that

he was a big fan of alligator chunks. "Come on, let's go and play in the garden."

"Glug loves chasing big sticks!" squawked Pummice, squeezing the tip of his tentacles into two padlocks and throwing open the back door. "You'll find plenty of big sticks in the shed, Nelly. Help yourself."

Nelly gave Glug a pat on the head and followed Pummice and Scroot back down the hallway in the direction of the purple bucket. "Mind the wallpaper paste!" said Nelly as the Grerks approached the front door.

"Oh that will be set solid by now," squawked Pummice.

Nelly peered into the bucket. Sure enough, the pea-green slop had totally transformed itself into a transparent lump of diamond-hard resin.

"Awesome!" thought Nelly. "I'll have to pour some on Asti's cornflakes."

"We'll be back by eight o'clock Nelly," squawked Pummice and Scroot, slipping out of the front door in a flurry of goodbye tentacles. "Don't forget, alligator chunks at seven!"

"I won't forget, I promise," said Nelly with a wave. She watched the Grerks stomp down the front garden path and then closed the front door behind them.

"What on earth am I going to do now?" she murmured. "How am I going to entertain a *gog* for two hours?" She turned back in the direction

of the hallway to find Glug jumping up and down in eager anticipation, his toenails clattering against the floorboards like dominoes being shuffled.

"OK, Glug," smiled Nelly, "where are those big sticks?"

4

The Grerks's back garden looked much the same as Nelly's, except for the craters where Glug had been digging. In odd parts the lawn looked more like a bomb site, but in other places strange and exotic flowers flourished in abundance. Nelly skipped down the garden past some six-headed dandelions and rattled the door of the Grerks's wooden shed.

Entry was gained by the lifting of a simple latch. Nelly craned her neck cautiously inside, just in case there were any surprises lurking behind the door.

There were. The sticks weren't sticks at all. They were branches, tree trunks even – huge great things flown in by a Scandinavian monster company called *GogToys Direct*. Each branch was stacked neatly in one corner of the shed.

Nelly took a deep breath and wrapped her arms around the middle of a branch that had been stacked neatly in one corner of the shed. With a grunt and a gasp, she tugged it in the direction of the five tails that were wagging uncontrollably behind her.

The "stick" weighed a ton and felt like a telegraph pole pressing against her shoulder as she pulled it free. Nelly's cheeks puffed full and fat and her face turned Wizzil-eye red, as slowly and unsteadily she inched the branch towards the lawn.

Glug's eyes bulged with excitement and his six scaly legs began to yo-yo on the spot. Nelly came out of the shed backwards, finding it easier to tug than to push. With a weightlifter's wince she composed herself for a moment and then inched the flats of her hand as far up the branch as she could reach.

Glug bounded up the lawn with his orange tongues flapping, made an unexpected handbrake turn by the patio doors and waited excitedly for Nelly to throw the stick to him.

Nelly blinked apologetically in Glug's direction and heaved the branch like a dead weight on to the ground. "Fetch," she gasped.

For a moment Glug seemed confused. This was a variation of a familiar game that he hadn't played before. He cocked his head to one side, yo-yoed up and down two or three times and then, with a wolfish, snarling growl, hurtled back down the garden in the direction of the stick.

Nelly jumped back in alarm as Glug's jaws clamped down ferociously onto the branch and his head began to shake. His jaws shook with such force his two orange tongues actually blurred into one. In a slobbering slavering frenzy of snarls he reduced the branch to sawdust.

Nelly stood motionless in the garden for a moment, trying to banish thoughts of what jaws like that could do to her legs should Glug become prematurely peckish. With a twist of her wrist she peered down at her watch. It was 6:45.

"Alligator chunks. Alligator chunks in fifteen minutes," she smiled. "Good gog, Glug. Smart gog, Glug!" she said, stepping forward confidently and rewarding him with a pat on the head.

Glug padded playfully through the sawdust and cocked his head in the direction of the shed. He understood the game now and wanted to play some more. Nelly knelt down beside him and draped her arms wearily around his neck.

"Sorry Glug, I'm tired. Let's play something else."

Glug began to circle Nelly's feet as Nelly racked her brains for something to do.

"I know!" she thought. "We'll do commands! If he's a show dog he's bound to be good at commands!"

Nelly straightened her back, arched her eyebrows and pointed sharply at the ground with her newly elected "command finger."

"Sit!" she ordered. "Sit, Glug!"

Glug double licked her command finger and began bouncing around on all sixes.

Nelly withdrew her finger sharply and stuck it under her armpit to remove the slobber.

"Roll over!" she said, electing to use a full, five-fingered "command hand" this time.

Glug's orange tongues flicked out to greet her, but this time Nelly was quick to keep her hand above slobber height.

She raised her hand above Glug's head and repeated the command with a sequence of barrelling, turning wrist motions. Glug watched with interest and then sprang up in an attempt to reward Nelly with another lick.

Nelly sprang back. This wasn't working at all. She scratched her head. If "sit" didn't work and "roll over" didn't work then she was pretty sure she'd be wasting her time with "beg." And they were the only doggy commands that she knew.

She looked around the garden and then stared at the shed. There were no balls to throw; maybe she should try another stick. On the other hand, maybe she shouldn't. The very thought of lugging another branch out of the shed made her go weak at the knees. She looked at Glug and scratched her head again.

"Umm," she pondered. Scroot and Pummice had said Glug was a *Golden Revolver* so that must mean one of two things. "Either he fires bullets like a revolver..."

Nelly scratched her head.

"Or..."

She decided to chance it...

"Revolve!" she said, circling the air with her command finger.

To her amazement Glug's response was immediate. He sat down instantly at Nelly's feet and stared back up at her with blazing green show-gog eyes. With his tongues dangling and Nelly's command still ringing in his ears he revolved his head full circle in one direction and then 360 degrees in the other.

Nelly gulped. She really hadn't been expecting that! "Good gog," she gasped, dropping to her knees again and offering up both her cheeks for a double lick. "You are a clever boy, aren't you!"

Glug wagged his tails wildly enthusiastically and treated Nelly to a few more courtesy revolutions.

"Now for your reward!" laughed Nelly, pointing her command finger at the kitchen. "Come on, Glug. Alligator chunks!"

Glug howled like a wolf, sprang to his feet and began chasing all five tails at once.

"He must really like alligator chunks!" thought Nelly, hurrying up the garden with Glug nipping playfully at her heels.

When she arrived in the kitchen she found Glug had bounded ahead and was already sitting by his bowl, staring unblinkingly up at the counter. Nelly picked up the can opener and attached it to the lip of the can. With every twist of the handle, Glug's head swivelled like a light house.

"He *definitely* likes alligator chunks!" smiled Nelly, springing back from the dangle of slobber that was hanging from his chin.

With a curious frown, she removed the lid from the can and gave it a sniff. It smelt like cheesy feet mixed with bad eggs. She read the label: *Prime chunks of alligator from the smelliest swamps of Florida squashed into a rank rattlesnake jelly make GOODGOG alligator chunks the choice of champions. Best before Sep.08, 3004.*

Nelly held her nose, bent down and picked up Glug's bowl. Holding her breath momentarily she placed the bowl on the kitchen counter and turned the can upside down. The contents belched into the bowl like an avalanche of frogspawn. Nelly grimaced, placed the bowl on the floor and jumped back.

Bow bobbing, tails wagging, he gobbled each meaty chunk into slobbery oblivion. Before Nelly could even say "can opener" the bowl was empty and Glug was pushing it around the kitchen floor in two directions with his tongues.

Nelly jumped up on to the kitchen counter for safety, just in case he fancied her ankles as dessert.

After five saliva-filled minutes, both of Glug's

tongues finally gave up. With a double lick of his chops and a multi-wag of his tails he trotted outside into the garden. Nelly jumped down, re-trieved the bowl and watched from the kitchen window as he scuttled down the lawn and began sniffing round the trunk of an extremely large oak tree. He circled the tree three times and then cocked three legs at once. Not one leg. Not two legs, but three legs at once. Without losing his balance!

Nelly watched in amazement and then began to feel a little embarrassed. After all, Glug was about to have a very private moment and here

47

she was gawping at him from the kitchen window. She looked away, but her curiosity immediately got the better of her. How many sprinkles was it going to be? One, two or three? Her eyes pinged back to the base of the oak tree but before she could discover the answer, the sound of the front door bell pinged her head in the opposite direction.

Nelly looked towards the hallway. Perhaps the Grerks had come home early?

Although she doubted it, she had no choice but to leave Glug to his sprinkles and answer the door. Wiping her hands on her sweatshirt, she hurried back through the living room and into the hallway.

When she opened the front door she found not a Grerk, but a rather frail looking woman in a grey tweed skirt and white blouse, smiling at her. She was standing on the step and had a wicker basket hooked over her left arm and a small yellow and black striped envelope in her right hand.

"Hello," said the woman, "I'm sorry to bother you but I'm collecting on behalf of the Royal Society for the Prevention of Cruelty to Wasps. I posted an envelope through your letter box earlier in the week."

Nelly looked down at the envelope that the woman was waving in front of her nose.

"I don't actually live here," explained Nelly, "I'm just monster sitting for a couple of hours."

The charity worker's face pinched with disappointment. Nelly looked into the woman's basket at the one and only sealed envelope that she had managed to collect so far.

"Wait a moment," said Nelly, her face illuminating, "I think I know exactly where the Grerks have left their envelope. I'm sure I saw it on the mantelpiece in the living room!"

The charity worker's face brightened.

"If you'll excuse me for a moment I'll go and get it!" said Nelly.

Nelly left the charity worker on the doorstep for a moment. She threaded her way down the hallway, past the purple bucket, past the pasting table and the hairy wallpaper rolls and into the living room.

"The Grerks must love wasps!" she thought to herself, taking the *RSPCW* envelope from the shelf and feeling the weight of all the coins inside.

"I've found it!" she called out to the charity worker, clonking her way back across the floorboards, past the silver dust sheets, spotty paint tins and slimy fabric books. "It was on the mantelpiece in the living roo—?"

Nelly stopped dead in her tracks. The charity worker was nowhere to be seen.

"Where did she go?" puzzled Nelly, swivelling her head in all directions and doing a passable impression of a Golden Revolver.

The answer came from ankle height. A soft whimpering groan drew Nelly's eyes downwards to the garden path. The charity worker was lying there, flat out on her back, and her wicker basket was hanging from a rose bush.

Nelly stared down at her and then gasped. Plastered across the woman's white cotton blouse were the six muddy footprints of a rather large gog.

Glug had escaped through the open front door!

"It went thataway!" groaned the charity worker with a groggy glance down the path.

Nelly leapt from the step, hurdled the woman's outstretched body and raced to the end of the path. Her head flashed left and right in both directions but Glug was nowhere to be seen. With

Glug had escaped through the open front door!

a sick, uneasy feeling, Nelly trudged back up the path to the house and helped the charity worker to her feet.

"He was only playing," explained Nelly. "He's a Cutey Pie really."

The charity worker dropped her wicker basket into the nearest litter bin and staggered in the direction of home.

"What have I done?" gasped Nelly, sitting crestfallen on the front step. "I left the front door open. That makes it my fault. What am I going to do now?"

5

Panic, was the answer. Panic, run up and down Sweet Street in all directions waving her arms and shouting "GLUG GLUG GLUG!" at the top of her voice.

Heads turned and people frowned, but there was no sign of Glug anywhere. Glug the Pedigree Best of Breed Champion of Champions Golden Revolver that was being entered at Grunts the very next day complete with new collar and bow, was gone.

It was a disaster.

Nelly returned to number 55 and sat miserably on the front garden wall. She looked at her watch. It was twenty past seven. Pummice and Scroot would be back in forty minutes. How was she going to get Glug back in time? She needed help, but she couldn't ask her mom or dad. They'd never be able to get their heads around a gog with a revolving head. And she certainly couldn't trust Asti.

Nelly walked back inside the house and pulled her cell phone out of the front pocket of her jeans. All was not lost. She'd call Grit and Lump, her monster friends from number 42 and number 93. There was hope yet, if a Huffaluk and a Dendrilegs came to help her.

Grit and Lump didn't have far to come. When they heard the trouble that Nelly was in, the doors of number 42 and number 93 crashed open simultaneously. Lump was the first to hurdle the purple bucket and Grit came thundering up the hallway of number 55 seconds after.

They found Nelly in the kitchen, anxiously twiddling the handle of the can opener.

"I've looked everywhere," she sighed.

Grit patted Nelly's head with his three furry paws. "Don't worry. He must be somewhere, Nelly," he growled, "and if he's somewhere, we'll find him."

"I've got an idea," slurped Lump with a suckery thwuck. "Why don't we open another couple of tins of alligator chunks! Glug could smell an alligator chunk from ten streets away! If that doesn't attract him back, nothing will!"

Nelly knew a good idea when she heard one and this was a good idea. In fact it was better than a good idea, it was a Champion of Champions Idea!

"Where do the Grerks keep their gog food?" asked Grit. Nelly's command finger pointed urgently to the cupboard. "Up there," she said.

Grit opened the cupboard and ran a red hairy paw along the top shelf. His solitary eye, on the end of his long stalk feeler, periscoped up into the cupboard to confirm the worst. There was no gog food on the shelf. Nelly had used up the last can.

Nelly clasped her hands to her head. "I forgot!" she groaned. "The Grerks said they needed to buy some more gog food too. Bow, collar and gog food, that's what they've gone to buy. *Now* what are we going to do?"

Lump and Grit began opening all the cupboard doors. But nothing could be found that was remotely in the same smelly league as a can of alligator chunks.

"We'll just have to go searching for him," slurped Lump. "I'll do the odd numbers; you do the even numbers, Grit. Nelly, you stay here in case Glug comes home."

Nelly paced up and down in the kitchen as her two great friends hurried down the path in search of Glug.

She looked at her watch again. It was half-past seven. The minutes were whizzing by. The Grerks would be home in thirty minutes with a new bow and a new collar for a gog that was nowhere to be seen.

All Nelly could do was wait. And hope.

She stared down the garden from the kitchen window. She thought about the sticks and the games they had played together. She longed wistfully for the sight of those two orange tongues and would have given anything to be covered from head to toe with Glug slobber.

"He'll never come home," she sighed, removing the gog bowl from the sink and drying it with a towel. "He's had his dinner, why *should* he come home?"

Nelly didn't know why, but her prayers were miraculously answered almost the moment she placed the bowl on the drainer. With the clatter of the purple bucket and a wild scurry of claws, the pasting table in the hallway suddenly collapsed, the rolls of furry wallpaper scattered in all directions and a six-legged monster suddenly skidaddled into the kitchen, scooted past Nelly's legs and hid in the cupboard under the sink. Glug was back!

Nelly hardly had time to catch her breath before the bucket and the pasting table clattered again under the big hairy paws and suckery thwuckery tentacles of Grit and Lump.

"He's back!" cried Nelly in delight. "Glug has come home!"

"We know," gasped Grit, "we saw him jumping over the fences, heading for home."

"Where's he gone?" squeaked Lump with a breathless thwuckthwuckthwuck.

Nelly crouched down by the cupboard under the sink and made calm reassuring noises in Glug's direction. Glug cowered out of sight with all five tails between his legs.

"Oh look he's hurt his nose," Nelly said, peering

tenderly into the cupboard. Grit and Lump stooped low to inspect the damage.

"It's only a scratch," growled Grit.

"It's not even a scratch," thwucked Lump.

"Who did that to your nose, Glug?" said Nelly gently. "It's all right, you can come out now. You're home where you belong and mommy and daddy will soon be home too with a nice new bow and collar for you to wear to tomorrow's show."

"I'll shut the front door in case he tries to run off again," growled Grit.

"I'll tidy up the hallway," thwucked Lump.

"Good idea," said Nelly.

Lump and Grit left Nelly to coax Glug out of the cupboard. When they returned to the kitchen they found Nelly with her head in her hands.

Glug was sitting on the furry carpet tiles scratching his hind quarters with both back legs at once. Although Glug showed no signs of going anywhere, his coat was on the move. It was teeming, it was wriggling, it was completely alive with fleas.

"Oh dear," growled Grit, "he's been sniffing around the mongrowl at number 252."

"What's a *mongrowl?*" asked Nelly.

"It's like a mongrel, only with more growl," explained Lump. "A *lot* more growl, actually."

Nelly gulped. She'd never seen fleas like these! They were as big as M&M's, as spiky as hedgehogs, as bouncy as superballs and there were hundreds of them!

"We've only got twelve minutes to get rid of them!" cried Nelly, staring goggle eyed at her watch.

"Run the bath, fetch the soap!" roared Grit, picking Glug up in his red furry arms and carrying him up the stairs to the bathroom. "If there's one thing gog fleas hate, Nelly, it's soap!"

Nelly and Lump followed Grit hurriedly up the stairs. There was no time to lose. Nelly emptied a gallon drum of bubble bath into the biggest bath she'd ever seen while Lump turned on the faucet and rammed in the plug.

Grit waited for the water to rise then winced as Glug planted an affectionate tongue on both of his red hairy cheeks.

"He likes you!" chuckled Nelly.

"No time for that sort of nonsense," growled Grit, lowering Glug into the glistening cauldron of suds.

The result was extraordinary. Everyone ducked as the gog fleas exploded like gunpowder from Glug's shaggy coat and clung fast to the ceiling and walls of the bathroom.

"It's worked, Grit! It's worked, Lump! The moment they feel the soap, they jump!" cheered Nelly.

Grit smiled and heaved Glug from the bath, completely free of fleas.

"Look out!" cried Nelly, shielding her eyes, "they're jumping back!"

It was true. The very instant that Glug was lifted from the bath, the gog fleas leapt back on to his coat.

"Put him back in!" thwucked Lump. Grit duly

Once again the gog fleas exploded from his coat.

obliged and once again the gog fleas exploded from his coat.

"Take him back out!" cried Nelly.

Grit lifted Glug from the bathwater only to see him immediately attacked again by the fleas.

"Put him back in!"

"Take him back out!"

"Put him back in!"

"Take him back out!"

It was hopeless. Inside the tub all was well. But outside of the bath, away from the soap suds, Glug was an unstoppable flea magnet.

"Carry him out into the garden!" thwucked Lump. "We can hose him down with soapy water outside!"

Grit tumbled down the stairs with flea-ridden Glug in his paws, Nelly and Lump racing behind them.

Grit placed Glug in the middle of the lawn while Lump used all four tentacles at once to shampoo, lather, hose and rinse Glug's coat. Once again the gog fleas exploded from Glug's coat, this time gaining refuge in the surrounding trees and shrubs. But just as before, they imploded back onto his coat the moment Glug had shaken himself down.

Grit shook his head and growled, Lump closed all four eyes and suckerythwucked, Nelly leapt into the air and whooped!

"Quickquickquick!" she cried. "I've got an idea! Bring Glug into the living room, we're going to do some decorating!" Grit and Lump didn't ask questions. There was far too little time for questions.

Nelly ran through the kitchen, grabbing a bottle of liquid soap on the way. "We need a bucket, the purple one's no use – try and find a bucket – THE BIGGER THE BETTER!"

Grit handed Glug to Lump, ran outside into the back garden and came back with a wheelie bin under one of his arms.

"Perfect!" said Nelly, pushing the silver-foiled furniture into the middle of the room. She looked at her watch. The Grerks would be home in six and a half minutes!

"OK," said Nelly. "We need to mix lots of wallpaper paste and fast!" Lump took charge, handing Glug back to Grit and ripping six packets of paste open with one tentacle, pouring them into the wheelie bin with another tentacle and adding water and stirring the mixture into a green slimy slop with his two other tentacles.

"You can never have too many tentacles," thought Nelly, handing out five large paste brushes and four paint rollers. "I want the ceiling and walls pasted from top to bottom, quick as quickquickquick!" she pleaded.

Grit handed Glug to Lump, Lump handed Glug back to Grit, Grit turned to Nelly and decided it was high time he put Glug back down on the floor.

All nine hands set to work. "Four minutes!" warned Nelly as a blur of tentacles and furry paws whizzed green sloppy goo across the walls and above her head.

"You've missed a bit," thwucked Lump, throwing a four-eyed perfectionist glance at

Grit.

"Never mind that!" shouted Nelly, raising the bottle of soap and aiming it directly at Glug.

She squeezed hard and then jumped back as the longer lasting lemon fresh formula spurted all over his coat. Once again the gog fleas exploded from Glug's coat and clung to the ceiling and walls. Only this time that's precisely where they stayed, welded into place by the quick drying Monsta-Paste!

"We're not finished yet!" shouted Nelly, handing out the lemon and black spotty paint tins. "Ceiling and walls please, in double quick time!"

Grit and Lump duly obliged, slapping and sploshing lemon and black spots in all directions fast. Grit was particularly careful not to "miss a bit" this time. He couldn't help feeling a little stung by the earlier criticism but consoled himself with the fact that Lump's four-tentacle advantage over his three paws made it perfectly reasonable to miss a bit anyway. In fact a lesser Huffaluk would probably have missed lots of bits.

While Lump and Grit started with the paint rollers, Nelly went to work with a hairdryer, drying and buffing Glug's coat back to a show gog standard of presentation. She still didn't know why Glug had run home, but she was so so happy that he had. She waved the hairdryer through his bow once more and leant back to admire the results. He looked perfect. A true Champion of Champions. Apart from perhaps that little mark on his nose.

But there was something she could do about that too. "Can I borrow your paint can a minute please Grit?" Nelly asked.

"I haven't missed a bit, have I?" he growled.

Nelly laughed and shook her head. "No, but I have!" She peered into the can and carefully placed the tip of her finger into the middle of an oily black circle of paint. With delicate precision she carefully dabbed her fingertip on to the tip of Glug's nose.

"Perfect. Glug, you're as good as new!"

"We're done!" growled Grit triumphantly.

"Do you want us to wash the brushes?"

"There isn't time!" laughed Nelly. "I want you to run down the garden path as fast as you can and disappear before the Grerks come home!"

It was one minute to eight.

"Consider us gone, Nelly," said Lump with a suckery thwuck.

"WATCH THE BUCKET AND THANKS FOR YOUR HELP!" shouted Nelly.

Lump and Grit raced out of the house as fast as they had raced in. Although this time taking especially good care to close the front door behind them.

Nelly flopped out onto the silver foil covering the sofa and was enthusiastically joined by Glug. With a puff of her cheeks and a slump of her shoulders, Nelly gazed around at the newly decorated ceiling and walls.

"I hope they like it," she said with an anxious nibble of her lip.

When the Grerks came home, they didn't like it. They loved it!

"I thought we'd go spiky wriggly in here," said Nelly, pointing to the curious texture of the ceiling and walls.

"How original! How unusual! How creative, Nelly!" squawked Pummice. "We really are most impressed."

Scroot peered a little closer. "Are all my eyes deceiving me Nelly, or are the yellow and black spots actually wriggling?"

"It does sort of give that effect, yes," nodded Nelly.

"And you've shampooed Glug as well! How kind!" cried Pummice. "He's all ready for tomorrow's show! You really didn't have to do that as well!"

"Oh I did, believe me I really did," smiled Nelly.

Nelly stayed a few extra minutes at number 55 to see Glug crowned with his sparkling new silver collar and topped off with his new golden bow.

Three shakes of a Squiddl's belly button later, Nelly was closing the garden gate and heading back along Sweet Street in the direction of home.

"YOU'RE AN INTERIOR DESIGN GENIUS, NELLY!" squawked Pummice and Scroot, waving their tentacles vigorously from the door.

Nelly turned and waved back.

"THAT'S ME!" she laughed, raising a can of lemon and black spotty paint above her head. "Thanks for this! I'll redecorate my bedroom soon!"

"You're very welcome!" squawked the Grerks.

Nelly breathed a huge sigh of relief and turned for home.

"That was a close call!" she sighed.

6

Whenever Nelly returned home from her crazy, heart-stopping monster-sitting adventures there was always a moment of readjustment. It was like stepping off a roller coaster and suddenly being rocked by the steadiness of the ground around her. The walls, the furniture, her family's voices, the sounds of the television, everything about number 119 was so quietly and reassuringly normal. Even after the funniest, gunkiest, loopiest, gloopiest monster-sitting adventures, Nelly was never sorry to be home.

This evening, she had her favorite pizza combo to look forward to. So what would be waiting to greet Nelly when she returned? Would it be a thin crust? Or would it be deep dish?

It would be chaos.

For no apparent reason Asti had gone off on one. She was hysterical, out of control, stamping her feet and waving her arms as only Asti could.

"I DID SEE IT!" she was screaming. "I DID I DID I DID!"

Nelly's mom and dad were trying to calm Asti down with a slice of Caribbean pizza with extra pineapple. But the more they waved it in front of her face, the angrier she got.

"IT JUMPED STRAIGHT OVER OUR FENCE, RIGHT OVER NEXT DOOR'S HEDGE! IT WAS HUGE! IT WAS HIDEOUS!"

Nelly left her cheese and chillie pizza in its box for a moment and listened intently to Asti's outburst. After all, it wasn't often that her sister had something interesting to say.

Asti, sensing a potential ally, shared her frustration with Nelly.

"Nelly, I bet you know what it was. It's probably one of your revolting friends. It had ten legs *at least* and it must have been the size of a rhinoceros," she exaggerated.

Nelly looked at her mom. Her mom looked at her dad. Everyone looked at the Caribbean pizza slice.

"I'M TELLING YOU IT WAS STANDING OUT THERE IN THE GARDEN OVER BY THE RABBIT HUTCH!" shrieked Asti. "IT HAD TWO ORANGE TONGUES, AT LEAST TEN TAILS AND ITS FACE WAS PRESSED RIGHT UP CLOSE TO THE WIRE!... AND AND... AND IT HAD A BLUE RIBBON ON ITS HEAD!"

Nelly reached for her pizza box and peered inside. It was deep dish.

"YOU MUST KNOW WHAT IT WAS NELLY!" shrieked Asti. "YOU MUST!"

Nelly sunk her teeth through a hot chilli and shook her head slowly. "Are you sure it wasn't a badger?" she asked with a straight face.

"A BADGER?" squealed Asti. "BADGERS DON'T JUMP FENCES! BADGERS CAN'T HOWL LIKE A PACK OF WOLVES!"

"A fox then?" suggested Nelly helpfully.

Asti exploded, slapping the Caribbean pizza slice

out of her mom's hand, banging the box on the kitchen counter and stomping upstairs to her room.

Nelly's dad opened Asti's pizza box, picked out all the bits of ham and added them to his Meat Feast.

"Maybe she's tired," said Nelly.

Nelly's mom broke from her Asti-induced stupor and shook her head in bewilderment.

"How were the Grerks? Did you have a nice time, love?"

"I had a great time thanks," said Nelly thoughtfully.

Later that evening, before heading to her room to write her notes, Nelly offered to put the empty pizza boxes in the recycling bin outside. On the short trip back across the patio, she stopped to talk to a friend.

"Hello beautiful," she whispered. "Do you know something I don't know?"

Snowball took time out from a cabbage leaf, hopped across the hutch and pressed his soft pink nose against the wire wall of his cage.

"You didn't by any chance meet a gog called Glug today did you? And you didn't by any chance nip him on the nose did you? And you're not by any chance the reason that Glug ran all the way home to me are you, Snowball?"

Snowball flopped his ears to one side and stared indifferently through the wire.

"I owe you, Snowball," whispered Nelly.

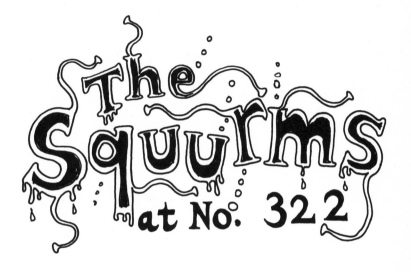

1

Nelly and Asti were arguing again. Not about music or TV shows or the meaning of life. This time it was something far more important. This time it was syrup.

"I got it first," snapped Asti.

"I took it out of the cupboard in the first place!" countered Nelly.

The golden syrup lurched backwards and forwards across the kitchen table as both sisters wrestled for control of the tin.

"If you don't stop arguing I'll tip the rest of this mix down the sink and there won't be any more pancakes for anyone!" threatened Nelly's mom.

Nelly's dad wiped some sugar from the corner of his mouth and groaned.

"But that's not fair! It's not me, it's them. I

haven't even *touched* the golden syrup, I've just had sugar and lemon on mine."

Nelly's mom paddled her wooden spatula through the pancake mix and sighed.

"Honestly, Clifford, sometimes I wonder who the biggest kid in this family is."

"They're bigger kids than me," said Dad, folding his arms indignantly and watching the golden syrup tin ping pong backwards and forwards in front of his eyes.

"Petronella and Astilbe Morton!" (Mom always called the twins by their full names when she was angry.) "If one of you girls doesn't give in, both your pancakes will go stone cold and then no amount of golden syrup will make them edible!"

"I'm not giving in," grimaced Nelly.

"I'm not giving in," growled Asti.

The twins tightened their grips on the golden syrup tin and prepared to battle right through the afternoon and into the night.

"I wish there was no such thing as Pancake

Day," grumbled Mom, ladling another dollop of pancake mix into the frying pan. "Instead of Pancake Day, there should be Twins Go To Bed Early Day or Moms Go Shopping and Spend However Much They Want To Day."

"Can I volunteer for the next pancake please, love?" asked Dad hopefully. "I mean, the girls haven't even started to eat their first one yet."

Mom flopped the pancake onto her husband's plate and looked despairingly at her two daughters.

"Smelly Nelly," lurched Asti.

"Nasty Asti," lurched Nelly.

"Could you fetch the jam, dear, I think I'd really like jam on this one," chimed Dad.

Nelly's mom was just about to pour the rest of the pancake mix over her family's heads, pack her bags and start a new life in Hawaii when the phone rang.

Not the phone in the hallway downstairs, but the phone in Nelly's bedroom upstairs.

Although it sounded faint from the kitchen, Nelly's monster-sitting phone had a very distinctive trilling ring. And when it rang it only ever meant one thing. Nelly was in demand.

Nelly's eyes detached themselves from the golden syrup tin and craned upwards to the ceiling. How could she answer the phone in her bedroom without giving control of the golden syrup to Asti?

The phone continued to ring unanswered.

Asti sensed victory. "Your phone is ringing, Nelly my sweet," she cooed, "and if you don't answer it pretty soonish one of your scummy hideous ten-headed monster friends won't be able to go out tonight and leave you with one of their freaky monster babies."

Nelly bit her lip, shoved the tin of golden syrup into Asti's chest and raced out of the kitchen and up the stairs. As she burst through her bedroom door she was greeted by the sound of her own voice.

"Please leave a message after the beeps and I'll get back to you as soon as I can."

Instead of diving for the phone, Nelly's curiosity got the better of her. She sat down at her homework table with her fingers poised over the phone and waited for the beep to beep.

The beep of the answer phone was followed by a *gurgle* and then a low *googling glug*. Nelly listened intently as the monster on the end of the line began to leave its message.

"Er... hello Nelly... *gurgle*... Er, we're the Squurms from number 322... *gloog*... we haven't met before but we've... *glargle*... we've heard a lot of wonderful things about you from Momp and Leech at number 93... *glurg*... We were wondering if you might be able to monster sit for us this evening?"

Nelly picked up the phone. "Hello?" she smiled.

Two loud *gurgles* were followed by a *glug* and then a ning.

"Is that Nelly the Monster Sitter... *gurgle?*"

"That's me!" said Nelly. "Of course I'll monster sit for you this evening. What time would you like

me to come over?"

The gurgles googled and glurgled softly at the end of the phone and then returned full volume with the answer.

"Could you come at six-thirty and perhaps... *glargle*... stay until nine?"

Nelly glanced at her secret drawer and smiled. "I'll have to check with my mom and dad but if you don't hear from me I'll be there right on time. Do I need to bring anything special?"

"Lots of energy!" gurgled the Squurm. "Our son, *gloogle* gets bored rather easily."

"Is that your son's name, Gloogle?" asked Nelly.

"Pardon *gurgle*," said the Squurm.

"You said 'our son Gloogle' ... is Gloogle your son's name?"

"Our son's name is Slop *gloogle*," glugged the Squurm.

"Slopgloogle or just Slop?" asked Nelly, who was beginning to wish she hadn't asked.

"Just Slop *gurgle*," gargled the Squurm, a little confused.

"Oh I see, Slopgurgle not Slopgloogle," said Nelly, trying not to giggle.

"No – just Slop. Our son's name is Slop, no gurgles or gloogles, just Slop..." glurgled the Squurm.

"And my name's just Nelly!" laughed Nelly. "I'll see you this evening at six-thirty!"

Nelly put the phone down and opened the red diary on her desk. She removed a strawberry gel pen from her pencil case and carefully added *6:30 Squurms at number 322* to her monster-sitting diary. She closed the clasp, placed the pen back in its case and swivelled around in her chair. She was just about to lean forward in the direction of her secret drawer when she suddenly sat bolt upright in her chair.

"PANCAKES!" she gasped. Asti was in control of the pancakes!

There was no time to lose. A new entry in her secret monster-sitting notebook would have to wait! The wheels on the bottom of Nelly's office chair spun like a Pookle's eyeballs as she launched herself out of her bedroom, down the stairs and into the kitchen.

When she arrived back at the table she found to her dismay that Pancake Day was most definitely over. Her mom was washing up the frying pan, her dad was refilling the sugar bowl and Asti was licking the golden syrup spoon.

"It's all gone," Asti said with a triumphant lick of the spoon. "Gone gone gone" she said with three more hugely exaggerated licks.

Nelly's toes curled up inside her shoes. They had a habit of doing that when she was angry.

"You greedy pig!" she snapped at her sister. "That tin was half full!"

"Now it's two halves empty," smiled Asti.

Nelly looked at her plate. There was plenty of space and a distinct lack of pancake.

"I ate it before it got cold," smirked Asti. "Mom said I could."

"OH Mom!" protested Nelly, placing her hands on her hips and staring daggers at the back of her mom's apron.

"Don't you Oh Mom me," said her mom, plunging the mixing bowl into the soap suds. "What with golden syrup wars and 'get me the jam' I've had pancakes up to here!"

"Me too," smiled Asti pointing to her tummy. "Actually I've had pancakes up to here," she said, moving her hand five inches further up her jumper.

Nelly turned to her dad, but at the mention of jam, he had started limping again. Nelly's toes wouldn't curl any further and so with as much self control as she could muster she marched out of the kitchen and straight up to the hallway mirror.

"Where are you off to this time?" called her dad, responding to the squeaks of marker pen on Post-it pad.

"The Squurms at number 322," said Nelly, imagining the mirror was Asti's face and slapping the Squurm's telephone number onto it hard. "They want me there at six-thirty."

"Do you have any homework to do?" called her mom. "I don't but Asti does!" shouted Nelly, beginning to exact some sweet revenge.

"Don't you Oh Mom me!" said Nelly's mom, pointing Asti up the stairs in the direction of her own homework table. "Now go and do your homework."

"I hate Math," said Asti, stomping out of the kitchen. "It's bad enough having to do it at school let alone at home."

"Pretend it's golden syrup," said her mom. "Now go and get stuck."

As Asti trudged to the bottom of the stairs Nelly bounced into her bedroom and closed her door.

Her mind was in monster mode now. "I wonder what Squurms look like? I bet they're hairy. No, they sound slimy. Maybe they're scaly? Where's my purple gel pen? Where's my monster notebook? Has Mom ironed my sardine sweatshirt?"

"Monster lover!" said Asti, reaching for the handle of Nelly's bedroom door.

Nelly turned the key in the lock.

"Click!" was her only reply.

2

Nelly emerged from her bedroom at 6:15, hair tied back, green jeans, red sneakers, sardine sweatshirt. She glanced in the direction of her sister's bedroom and smiled at the sight of Asti sucking a pencil so hard that her eyebrows had joined in the middle.

"The answer is two," said Nelly. "One plus one equals two."

Asti removed the pencil and stuck out her tongue.

Nelly smiled.

When she reached the bottom of the stairs she found her mom and dad crouching on their knees and running their hands over the hallway carpet. "Watch your feet," said her mom. "Your dad's lost his contact lenses."

"They're in the bathroom in their case," said Nelly. "I saw them there ten minutes ago when I was washing my face."

Nelly's mom stood up with a sigh, while Nelly's dad stayed low and looked sheepish. "I could have sworn I had them in," he said. "I thought they'd both fallen out when I sneezed."

"We're both going to fall out in a minute, if you're not careful," growled Nelly's mom. Nelly laughed and opened the front door. She felt sorry for her dad sometimes. He always seemed to be one step away from a limp.

"I'll be back just after nine," she said.

"Have fun," said her mom.

"I'm going back to glasses," muttered her dad.

Nelly closed the front door and trotted cheerfully to the end of the garden path. There was a springtime springiness in her step, given extra bounce by the excitement of meeting some new monsters.

She closed the garden gate behind her and turned in the direction of the high, even house numbers. Number 322 was going to be some way up Sweet Street to her left. And she would need to cross the road to reach it.

She had decided to stay on this side of the road for most of the way and cross further up, but when she saw Natalie Dupre approaching in the distance she decided to cross early. Natalie Dupre was Asti's best friend and as far as Nelly was concerned, that made her someone to be avoided.

Nelly stopped at the curb and pretended not to notice Natalie approaching. But wouldn't you just know it, the very moment Nelly needed to cross Sweet Street the traffic became so busy in both directions that she became hopelessly rooted to the curb.

Nelly tried to glance sideways without moving her head. Natalie was a matter of feet away now and would open her Frisbee-sized mouth any moment. Nelly considered throwing herself under a bus, but decided that was a bit drastic.

"Hello, Nellsmell!" said Natalie. "Where are you off to?"

Nelly's head turned with painful reluctance in the direction of Natalie's snake lipped smile.

"Out," said Nelly.

"You're not going to baby sit one of those freaky deaky monster thingies are you? Asti says they've got twenty heads and huge fangs and no legs and they slime and gunge everywhere and all over the place. And they eat people, or chop you up into pieces with their razor sharp claws. I hope you've done karate. I wouldn't go anywhere near something like that unless I knew karate. Asti says sometimes if they're not hungry, instead of eating all of you they put giant straws in your ears and just suck your brains out instead."

"Asti should know," said Nelly.

"What do you mean?" asked Natalie, her eyes darkening with concern.

Nelly put on her most solemn face. "The first time I went monster sitting I took Asti with me. The monsters got a bit hungry and Asti got grabbed. I managed to hide under the table, but Asti wasn't so lucky. I actually had to watch as they sucked her brains right out."

Natalie clasped her hands over her mouth in horror. "Really?!" she gasped.

"That's why she can't do Math," said Nelly, trying to keep a straight face. "She's got no brain."

Natalie Dupre stood silently beside Nelly and then stared up the road at number 119. "What color was the straw?" said Natalie.

"Green and white stripy," said Nelly. "She's in her bedroom trying to do her homework now, maybe you could help her. Don't say that I told you about the brain removal, because she doesn't want anyone to know."

Natalie clasped Nelly's hands in hers and gave them a reassuring squeeze. "It will be our secret, Nelly," she whispered. "I promise I won't say a word."

"I've gotta go," said Nelly. "Or I'm going to be late."

"Me too," said Natalie, hurrying on to offer Asti

a lend of her brain.

Nelly waited for a lull in the traffic and then dashed across the road. She kept the momentum of the run going a full hundred feet further up Sweet Street, only slowing as she approached the low three hundreds.

312, 314, 316... no purple doors yet... 318, 320... 322. No purple door at all. In fact the front door of number 322 Sweet Street was plain ordinary white. If Nelly hadn't had a good reason to take a special interest in it, she would have passed it by without even a glance.

Nelly looked around the front garden for clues of monster inhabitants. The privet hedge was neatly clipped, the lawn was nicely kept. There were no two-headed garden gnomes in the borders and no giant milk bottles on the door step. When she pushed the front gate open, it creaked like an ordinary gate and when she walked down the garden path it felt like an ordinary garden path beneath her feet.

"I hope I haven't got the wrong house," she

thought to herself. "I'm sure they said 322."

Nelly glanced at her watch. It was 6:30 on the dot. "Oh well, fingers crossed," she sighed, smoothing her sweatshirt and reaching up to press the doorbell.

As she pressed the clear plastic button her fingertip sank down into it like a hippo in a swamp. The release of the button was followed by a loud squelch and then topped with the extraordinary sound of a toilet flushing.

Nelly smiled with relief. "This must be the right house!"

3

She was still smiling broadly when the front door flew open. Nelly's eyes widened as two monsters oozed into view. "Hello," gurgled the Squurm to her right. "My name's Dollop, and this is my wife Splat. You must be Nelly!"

"That's me!" said Nelly, holding out her hand but then withdrawing it quickly out of politeness. As far as she could see, the Squurms didn't have any hands to shake! They were like slugs. Giant orange upright slugs, with moist glistening bodies and wet foaming mouths. All over their heads soft yellow eyes nestled like egg yolks. And from their cheeks stiff black whiskers bristled like burnt sparklers.

They seemed very pleased to see Nelly. "Give us a squonk, Nelly the Monster Sitter!" gurgled Splat.

Nelly braced herself as two spaghetti-like feelers suddenly sprang from the Squurm's chest and planted themselves on Nelly's nose. Nelly's face tingled with cold as two more feelers sprung forward from Dollop's shoulders and fastened themselves to her cheeks. She'd never been kissed Squurm-style before. It was like having your face pressed into a bowl full of cold jelly.

Splat and Dollop finished with the yucky kissy squonky stuff and then began gurgling to one another with excitement. Nelly wiped her face discreetly with the back of her hand and smiled.

"Aren't you going to introduce me to Slop?" she laughed. "Of course we *gurgle* are!" replied Dollop, sprouting another spaghetti-like feeler and using it to beckon Nelly inside the house. "Please come through."

Nelly stepped into the hallway. The doormat was squelchy too. So was the hallway floor. Not sticky squelchy, more bouncy squelchy, sort of like walking around on a giant gummy bear.

Nelly bounced along the hallway behind the

Squurms and then glanced over her shoulder. "You've forgotten to close the front door," she said, pointing back to the front door.

"I'll get it," gurgled Dollop, sprouting a four foot long feeler and sending it through the air past Nelly's nose and in the direction of the open door.

The front door slammed with a squelch.

"Goodness!" thought Nelly, following Splat and Dollop into the living room. "Exactly how many feelers does a Squurm have?"

The answer was going up all the time. For there in the middle of the floor, sitting on a white rubber carpet was Slop. Orange, damp and glistening, Slop was juggling nine red bananas with six feelers, seven pink apples with five feelers and spinning an aluminium fruit bowl with another feeler. He was only about three feet tall, but what he lacked in height, he more than made up for in circus tricks.

"That's a lot of feelers," thought Nelly, losing count after fourteen. "And that is one clever little monster."

"Slop, this is Nelly the Monster Sitter!" gurgled Dollop. "Nelly has come to play with you."

A shower of monster fruit clattered on to the mat as Slop withdrew the tentacles back inside his body and began bouncing up and down like a space hopper.

"Ooh glood! Oh glood!" gurgled Slop, squirming excitedly into a froth of orange bubbles.

"Pleased to meet you, Slop," smiled Nelly.

"Come and sit next to us Nelly," gurgled Splat, patting a large green plastic sofa with her feeler. Nelly lowered her bottom on to the sofa and then toppled over as her bottom slid in three directions at once. "Is it full of water?" laughed Nelly, trying to settle on the sofa without bouncing too much.

Dollop laughed. "No, Kipple blubber. It's very comfortable, isn't it, Nelly!"

"Once your bottom eventually stops wobbling!" chuckled Nelly.

Dollop and Splat oozed a little closer and wrapped six affectionate tentacles around her shoulders.

"Now then Nelly the Monster Sitter, tell us all about yourself."

"Well," said Nelly, not sure there was much to tell. "I live at number 119 with my mom and dad and my twin sister."

"And do they have one head each like you?" asked Dollop politely.

Nelly thought about Asti for a moment and then nodded.

"And how long have you been monster sitting?" gurgled Splat.

"About six months," smiled Nelly. "I love monster sitting, it's so much fun."

"I can see why you would enjoy meeting normal monsters like us," googled Dollop, "but don't you find monsters with lots of heads a bit frightening?"

"Two heads are better than one, my mom always says!" smiled Nelly.

"I'm sure you wouldn't say that if you met a

Plook," gurgled Spat. "All those pink scales, and those green and yellow spikes."

"And their purple ears," added Dollop with a shudder. "Plooks give me the wibbles I can tell you."

"Never judge a Plook by its cover, I say!" laughed Nelly.

"You're a brave one, Nelly the Monster Sitter. I can see our little Slop will be in safe suckers."

"Hands," said Nelly, holding up ten fingers. "Humans say 'safe hands.'"

"Squurms say 'safe suckers,' but tonight, it will be safe hands!" gurgled Splat, waving two feelers playfully in front of Dollop's nose.

Nelly glanced down at her feet. Slop had slithered across the floor towards her and was playing with the laces of her sneakers. "How old is Slop?" whispered Nelly.

"He's five and a bite," googled Splat.

"Don't you mean five and a bit?" asked Nelly.

"No, his teeth have come through now. He's five and a bite. Show Nelly your teeth, Slop."

Slop tilted six yolky yellow eyes up at Nelly and parted his thin black inner-tube-like lips into a smile.

Two rows of lime-green barracuda style teeth presented themselves to Nelly.

"He may only be five and a bite," continued Splat, "but he's very advanced for his age. He can already count from a trillion to one backwards and he can do his eighty-three times table just like…"

Nelly leant back as Splat clicked another feeler in front of her nose… "that!"

Nelly smiled at Slop and then leant forward to examine her shoelaces. Slop had tied both of them together.

"Hah! So you're a practical joker, are you Slop?" laughed Nelly. "I'm not falling for that one!"

Slop's eyes glowed orange for a moment and then faded back to yellow.

"The trouble is, Nelly," gurgled Dollop, "because he's so bright, Slop gets SO bored SO easily. Do you think you'll be able to keep him amused while we're away?"

"Entertainment is my middle name!" smiled Nelly, retying her laces and then sliding off the sofa with a squelch. "We'll be fine won't we, Slop?"

"What are we gloing to play, Nelly?" gurgled Slop, his orange body rippling like a caterpillar.

"There are plenty of games in the cupboard under the window," gurgled Dollop.

Nelly sat cross-legged on the floor in front of Slop. She gave him a playful nudge with her elbow and peered deeply into three of his yolky eyes.

"It's far too nice an evening to play inside!" laughed Nelly. "I think we should go out into the garden, don't you, Slop? Maybe we can make up some games of our own!"

Slop began to froth with excitement, and pointed all six eyes in the direction of the garden.

Splat stood up with a blubbery squish.

"Dollop and I thought we'd go to the movies, Nelly," she gurgled. "We've never been to see a movie in a theater before! I'm just going upstairs to put on my makeup and then we'll be ready to leave."

Nelly adjusted her scrunchy and smiled. "We'll be outside if you need us," she said. "Come on, Slop. Show me where the garden is. It's time to have some fun!"

Before Nelly could blink, a long sinuous feeler sprouted from Slop's forehead and attached itself like a limpet to her chin.

"Thish way Nelly!" he frothed excitedly.

Nelly scrambled to her feet and let her chin do the leading. Across the soft rubbery white tiles of the living room she ran, through a glistening curtain of silver beads and into another room at the back of the house.

Nelly could see the garden beckoning through the open French doors, but suddenly applied the brakes. The soles of her sneakers squeaked as she skidded to a halt on the rubber carpet.

"Whoa Slop, whoa!" she laughed. "What have you got there?"

Slop squelched to an impatient halt and turned

round. His yellow yolky eyes travelled down the length of Nelly's outstretched arm and came to rest on the tip of her pointing finger.

"It's our fish tank," said Slop, releasing Nelly's chin with a soft thwuck. Nelly leant forward and peered wide eyed at the biggest home aquarium she had ever seen. It was at least six feet long and three feet deep, and it was supported by an industrial-strength stand made of scaffold poles.

"That glass must be five inches thick!" gasped Nelly, tapping the front wall of the aquarium with the back of her finger.

It needed to be. The moment Nelly's finger tapped the glass a shoal of ferocious yellow creatures flew out from behind a pile of yellow house bricks, hurled themselves in her direction and began barking at the glass.

Yes – *barking* at the glass.

Nelly withdrew her finger instantly and watched in astonishment as the barking turned to growls. She'd never seen or heard fish like

them. They were about the length of a fish stick, but there the similarities ended. Some had two heads, some had three tails and there was a distinct lack of breadcrumbs. Across the tops of their backs was a crest of black needles and along both flanks of their bodies were ridges of flapping red fins.

"What kind of fish are those?" Nelly gasped.

"Shreddas," yawned Slop.

"They look hungry," said Nelly, leaning forward for a closer inspection and then stepping back as the growls erupted into barks again.

"They're *always* hungry," sighed Slop.

"What do you feed them?" asked Nelly, taking another cautionary step away from the aquarium glass.

"Piranhas," yawned Slop. "Come on Nelly, fish tanks are boring. Let's go into the garden and play."

Nelly quivered slightly as another cold, damp Slop sucker attached itself to her right ear and drew her gently away from the aquarium.

Six sideways steps and a tug, and Nelly was through the French doors and into the garden.

"I'm telling you Slop, if you think shreddas are boring, you should try goldfish!" exclaimed Nelly. "Now goldfish are *really* boring."

Slop sprouted twelve sticky feelers, raised them to his mouth and yawned again.

"Be careful in the sandpit Nelly, it's very deep!" gurgled a familiar voice.

Nelly looked around and stifled a giggle. Splat was standing by the French windows sporting a kaleidoscope of yellow lipstick and green fluorescent eye shadow.

"It's glow in the dark makeup, Nelly! Do you think I'll look good at the movie theater?"

"I think you'll be a bigger attraction than the movie!" beamed Nelly. "I think you look stunning."

Splat's cheeks blushed blue with embarrassment. A twiddle of feelers rippled in all directions and then pointed in the direction of the lawn. "Seriously Nelly, please be very careful if you play in the sandpit. The sand goes all the way down."

Nelly followed Splat's feelers with her eyes and then smiled at the sight of a harmless looking circle of sand located in the middle of the lawn.

"It's OK, I've played in sandpits before!" laughed Nelly.

Dollop joined Splat and placed six feelers

affectionately around her waist. Or was it her neck? Or her knees? It wasn't easy to tell!

"It's time we went, dear," gurgled Dollop. "Or we'll miss the film."

"What are you going to see?" asked Nelly.

"Toxic Scum Revenge Attack III," gurgled Splat. "I do so love a good romance."

Nelly scratched her head and then smiled and waved.

"Don't forget to have an ice cream after!" shouted Nelly.

"I'm going to have six!" gurgled Dollop, waving back with a flurry of feelers. "We promise we'll be back by nine!"

Nelly watched the Squurms slither away and then return almost as quickly as they had gone.

"Nelly, there's one thing we forgot to tell you about playing games with Slop," gurgled Dollop.

"Oh yes, what's that?" smiled Nelly.

"Slop likes to win," gurgled Splat.

"Slop has to win!" gurgled Dollop.

"We'll see about that!" laughed Nelly.

4

The front door closed with a squelch and Nelly and Slop were left alone in the garden to play.

"Have you ever played bat and ball, Nelly?" gurgled Slop excitedly.

"Of course I have," said Nelly. "I'm pretty good at it actually."

"I bet I win!" gurgled Slop, bouncing straight down to the end of the lawn and wrenching open a pair of riveted steel shed doors. Nelly stood by the house and waited for Slop to emerge with a bat and ball.

The ball came first. It flew like a missile out of the shed without any warning at all and landed at her feet.

Nelly bent down and picked it up. It was made of clear plastic. It was as big as a soccer ball but rather oddly, it was as light as a ping-pong ball. There was something else that was strange about it too. It was full of winged insects, fluttering and flitting around inside. Nelly peered into the sphere for a closer look. It reminded her of a snow shaker except instead of snow there were creepy crawlies flying around.

They were like earwigs with wings. They had heads at both ends of a slender black body, pincer jaws and tiny silver eyes. Their wings extended in two directions at once from the middle of their body, allowing them to fly forward and reverse with ease.

Nelly shook the ball to stir them up a little and as she did so the ball began to buzz. The wings of the insects inside the ball blurred like humming-bird wings and the ball began to lift out of her hand.

"Wow!" thought Nelly. "This is one weird ball!"

Weird was about to get weirder.

Nelly was just drawing the ball back towards her chest when an almighty rumpus kicked up in the shed. It sounded like Slop was riding bucking bronco with a gorilla.

Nelly stared down the garden in amazement as Slop emerged partially from the darkness inside the shed and then catapulted back inside with a clatter.

He appeared again briefly, his orange feelers stretched tight and straining to drag something from the shed.

Twelve feelers, thirteen feelers, fourteen feelers sprung from his body, lassoing something inside.

Nelly covered her ears as a high pitched scream issued from inside the shed, sending the enamel on her teeth jangling. Whatever Slop had hold of didn't want to come out.

Another scream pierced Nelly's ear drums as Slop sent more tentacles into the darkness.

Slop was struggling, but he was winning. Inch by inch he was emerging from the shed, his whiskers bristling like a walrus and his feelers drawn tight as bicycle spokes.

"Just a sec, Nelly," he gurgled.

One explosive moment later, he was flat on his back on the lawn, buried beneath the crumpled wings of two very large and very angry bats.

"I've got them!" gurgled Slop. "They don't like playing games in the daylight!"

Nelly stared gobsmacked at the two bats that Slop had dragged from the shed. They had ultra violet eyes, flared, dragon-like nostrils, wings the texture of black velvet curtains and wingspans the size of hang gliders.

Slop extracted himself from the tangle, stood up and rippled with excitement.

"Choose a bat Nelly!" he gurgled.

With a slight intake of breath, Nelly pointed to the bat on the left. From where she was standing it looked the slightly smaller of the two.

"Good, I'll use this one then," gurgled Slop, attaching a sucker to the larger bat's nostril and leading it towards the house. Nelly's courage began to falter as the bat she had nominated to use stood up, flapped the creases from its wings and began lumbering grumpily across the lawn towards her.

"I wonder where the handle on my bat is?" she gulped, as Slop and the two bats joined Nelly at the top of the garden.

"OK Nelly, let's play!" gurgled Slop.

"Hold on," said Nelly, "I haven't played this kind of bat and ball before. You need to explain the rules!"

Slop let go of his bat's nostril and took the plastic sphere from Nelly's hands.

"This is a ball, Nelly. And these are the bats," gurgled Slop.

Nelly sighed. "Yes, Slop. I figured that!"

A shadow fell across her eyes as both of the bats loomed towards the ball and began salivating at the sight of the insects inside. Brown dribble fell like chocolate sauce on to the grass, just centifeet from the toes of Nelly's sneakers.

Slop attached a sucker to the ball that Nelly had been holding and began spinning it like a basketball in front of her nose.

"What you have to do Nelly, is throw the ball to me, without my bat chomping it and I have to throw the ball to you without your bat chomping it."

Nelly nodded slowly. That sounded simple enough.

"The bats want to eat the insects inside the ball, so if you throw it too close to their jaws they'll munch it and crunch it. If my bat munches and crunches it on your throw, you lose. If your bat munches and crunches it on my throw, I lose."

"Are you ready to play, Nelly?" gurgled Slop, placing the ball between two suckers.

"I *think* so!" said Nelly, jumping backwards as her bat unfurled its monstrously big wings.

"One other thing I forgot to tell you, Nelly!" gurgled Slop.

"What's that!" squealed Nelly as the purple claws of her bat lunged unexpectedly for her shoe laces.

"It's an upside down game!"

Nelly squealed again as the talons of her bat

tightened around her laces, picked her up and swept her into the air. A flap and a swoop later she was upside down, dangling by two laces and staring at the roof tiles of the Squurms' house.

"Catch!" gurgled Slop.

Nelly glanced round dizzily. The roof tiles whizzed away as if she were on a roller coaster and she plummeted fast towards the ground.

"Catch Nelly!" gurgled Slop, waving the ball directly in front of her. Nelly threw out her arms as Slop released the ball from his suckers. Her brains felt like they were about to fall out through her ears.

The jaws of Nelly's bat snapped greedily as the ball

swerved first one way and then another before propelling itself into Nelly's outstretched palms.

"How did you get it to swerve?" she gasped, swooping back up and over the chimney.

"I didn't!" gurgled Slop. "The insects did it. They don't want to get eaten!"

"I don't blame them!" thought Nelly, trying to turn her eyeballs the right way up.

"Throw it to me Nelly," laughed Slop, dive bombing past the bathroom window.

Nelly swooned. Her brains had topsy-turvied and the blood in her veins was travelling south-north too. She hurled the ball as hard as she could in the direction of Slop's outstretched feelers, and then reached out unsuccessfully to try and steady herself on the drainpipe as she swooped past.

The eyes of Slop's bat glowed neon blue as the ball sped towards him. More chocolate sauce dribbled from its fangs and its lips rippled hungrily as the ball swerved close.

With a screech and swoop Slop's bat made its

move, lunging at the ball with wide open jaws. The heat from its nostrils steamed the surface of the ball as its fangs closed in on it. But as its jaws snapped shut, Slop's feeler whipcracked the ball away just in time.

"That was close Nelly! You'll have to throw harder than that!"

Nelly had already had enough. She was suffering badly from dangly-itis. In fact she doubted whether she would ever be able to stand up straight again.

Her bat still meant business though. It swooped left towards the fence, and right towards the shed where Slop was preparing to release the ball.

Slop was a master. He not only released the ball at just the right speed and at just the right time, but with just the right swerve to baffle her bat into missing. Nelly wasn't a master. She was a mess. She felt so dizzy she didn't know which way was pu and which way was nwod. But backwards and forwards they continued to swoop. As Nelly's hands closed around the ball for the seventh time she began to get the feeling that it wasn't the insects inside the ball that were buzzing, it was her brain cells. She felt giddy, she felt sick, she was completely dangled out. If she was going to find the energy to last until nine o'clock then there was nothing she could do. She would need to concede defeat. With a half-hearted loop of her arm she deliberately lobbed the ball tamely into the jaws of Slop's bat.

The plastic ball shattered and the insects scattered.

"I win!" gurgled Slop. "I always win."

Nelly groaned a sigh of relief as the wings of her bat stopped flapping and lowered her back down onto the lawn. She fell into a heap, rolled over and lay flat out on her back, staring up at the sky.

"One zero to me Nelly! Want to play again? I've got some more balls in the shed!"

Nelly shook her head, and tried to focus on a cloud, or a bird. Anything.

"I'll put the bats away then," gurgled Slop.

"Then we can play something else!"

As Slop led the bats back to the shed, Nelly flopped out and took the opportunity to try and catch her breath.

"You haven't got Wiffle Ball have you, Slop?" panted Nelly, lifting her head weakly and peering down the garden. "That's the sort of bat and ball game I like."

"The kids next door have," gurgled Slop. "I've watched them playing it from my bedroom window. It's a ball on a rope isn't it?"

Nelly nodded and then laughed as Slop sprouted a dozen feelers and pretended to play Swing Ball in front of her. Jumping from left to right and taking swipes at the air, he looked like a demented orange cheese string.

"I think Swing Ball would be better if it had a hundred balls on a hundred ropes!" gurgled Slop.

"You win again Slop!" laughed Nelly, conceding inevitable defeat.

Nelly sat up and looked up and down the garden. Playing games with a Squurm was proving more challenging than she had imagined. "Do you have any small buckets?" she said, looking optimistically at the sandpit in the middle of the lawn. "We can have a sand castle building competition."

Slop scratched his shins with three feelers. "I'm not sure it's the right sort of sand for sand castles," he gurgled.

"Don't worry," said Nelly. "If it's too dry, we can add some more water from the sink in the kitchen."

Nelly skipped down the garden in the direction of the sandpit. "Wow, I bet you have some fun in here, Slop!" she laughed.

"I haven't been in a sandpit for years!" she cried, throwing her arms above her head and jumping in with both feet.

Her legs vanished and the bones in her waist groaned as an unbearable pressure suddenly applied itself to her lower body. She was sliding fast. She was disappearing. Her ribcage felt like it was about to crunch like a walnut in a nut cracker!

"It's quicksand Slop! It's quicksand! I'm being sucked under, help me!"

Slop jumped into the sandpit and began to paddle around playfully on his back. For a Squurm it was nothing more than a paddling pool.

"I'm not playing Slop, I'm not playing! I'm sinking!"

"Oh gloodness!" gurgled Slop, sprouting thirty feelers all at once. Twelve slapped themselves to the top of Nelly's head, three fixed themselves to her cheek and nose, two more to her ears and the rest to a tree over by the fence.

With an incredible heave and a noise like a Bog belch, Nelly was dragged from the quicksand and dumped in a heap back on dry land.

She scrabbled to her feet, staggered left and right and brushed herself down.

"Thank you Slop!" panted Nelly. "That wasn't the sort of sand I was expecting! How deep does it go down?"

"Two miles is the furthest I've ever been," gurgled Slop. "Do you want me to get your socks and shoes?"

Nelly looked at her feet. Her socks and sneakers had been sucked clean off!

"Later," she gasped. "Slop, I hope you don't mind," said Nelly, stamping as much sand off as she could, "but I think we should play inside."

"I don't mind where we play, Nelly," gurgled Slop. "As long as I win!"

5

Nelly's bare feet padded across the white rubber flooring, past the shredda tank and back into the living room.

"I feel all stretched like a piece of elastic," said Nelly, doing a head over heels in the direction of the games cupboard.

"Who taught you to juggle?" said Nelly, picking up the red bananas and pink apples and returning them to the fruit bowl.

"I taught myself," gurgled Slop, cartwheeling on four feelers in the same direction.

"Can you do this with your tongue?" said Nelly, rolling her tongue like a newspaper and wiggling it about.

"I haven't got a tongue," gurgled Slop. "Can you do this with your eyes?"

Nelly watched as Slop jolted his head forward sharply, sending all six of his egg-yolk eyeballs dangling from their sockets. They bounced up and down in front of Nelly like globules of glue before catapulting back into place with another sharp flick.

"You're good!" grinned Nelly. "You're very good. But, can you do this?"

Slop watched intently as Nelly placed both hands behind her back, interlocked her fingers and then passed both hands back over her head again.

"I'm double jointed," smiled Nelly.

Slop grew eight feelers, twiddled them together like twine, passed them over his head, wrapped them around his waist and then draped them around his neck like a scarf.

"I'm no jointed," he grinned.

"You win!" laughed Nelly, somersaulting across the floor towards the games cupboard beneath the window.

"I always win!" boasted Slop.

"We'll see about that!" said Nelly, pushing open the two white plastic doors of the games cupboard. It was full of games. All of them monster strange.

"How do you play this?" asked Nelly, pulling a purple and red stripy box out of the cupboard.

"You need eight legs to play that one," gurgled Slop.

Nelly pushed the box back into place and yanked a long silver tube out from beneath it. Prying open the lid with her fingers, she tipped the tube in the direction of the floor and then watched in amazement. A six-legged dice was crawling to the lip of the tube. It jumped onto the carpet and began cart-wheeling across the floor. Nelly pressed her eye to the tube and then recoiled as hundreds of multi-colored tubes slithered like snakes onto the floor and began linking together to form different three-dimensional shapes.

"You need three feet to play that one," gurgled Slop, shooing the snakes and the dice back inside the tube. "And six noses."

127

Nelly returned the tube to the cupboard.

"How about this one?" asked Nelly, pulling a silver and green board game out of an aluminium box.

Slop oozed across the white rubber carpet and pressed his damp orange skin against Nelly's arm. Nelly's eyes followed a long spaghetti-like feeler as it emerged from Slop's forehead, wavered like a snail's horn through the air and finally came to a sticky rest on the bottom of the aluminium lid.

"Oh," said Nelly, reading the small print.

Not suitable for creatures with one brain.

"These are all monster games," gurgled Slop. "I'm afraid, Nelly, you have to be normal to play them."

Nelly sat up indignantly. "What are you saying, Slop? One head, two arms and two legs sounds perfectly normal to me!"

"Well not to me it doesn't!" gurgled Slop.

Nelly frowned into as many of Slop's eyes as she could see at once, held her breath for as long as she could, then burst out laughing.

"Haven't you got any normal games, sorry, I mean, *weirdo* games?" asked Nelly.

Slop scratched the middle of his chest with three feelers and thought hard. "Do you know what, Nelly? I believe there may be some weirdo games in the cupboard under the stairs. My mom bought a whole pile of weird stuff at a yardsale we went to last summer. I remember it was such a hot day we were asked to come off the bouncy castle. There was froth everywhere. We were in such a lather by the time we got home, Mom just threw the bags under the stairs and that's where they stayed."

"Let's take a look!" said Nelly.

Nelly followed Slop out of the living room and into the hallway. "They're in here," gurgled Slop, pointing to the base of the stairs. "There's no handle on the cupboard," said Nelly, running her fingers across the door.

"Squurms don't need handles," gurgled Slop, planting a sticky feeler pad against the chromium panel and wrenching it open with a thwuck.

Nelly waited patiently as Slop sent eight more feelers into the cupboard.

"Here they are," gurgled Slop, pulling three large carrier bags out of the darkness.

"Excellent!" said Nelly, dropping to her knees and plunging her hands inside the first bag. "Well, we can't play kettle and we can't play saucepan," said Nelly, rummaging through the contents. "Or flower pot or toasted-cheese maker or bread board. Let's have a look in the second bag."

Slop hurled the first bag back under the stairs while Nelly reached inside the second.

"TWISTER!" she cried. "You've got Twister! Oh, I love Twister. You'll love Twister!"

"How do you play Twister?" gurgled Slop, a little intrigued.

Nelly opened the box and explained. "Basically you spread this mat out on the floor like this, and you have to stretch your arms and legs across all these different colored circles and get in a big tangle without losing your balance. If you lose your balance and fall over, the other person wins!"

"I win again," gurgled Slop, once Nelly had laid out the Twister mat.

Nelly watched dumbfounded as Slop sprouted more feelers than a sea anemone and placed them effortlessly on every colored circle on the mat without losing his balance in the slightest.

"I can take your turns too if you like!" laughed Slop, doubling his feelers to twenty-four and then producing one extra feeler to tickle Nelly under the chin with.

Nelly folded the Twister mat and stuck it back in its box. "OK, maybe Twister isn't for us," sighed Nelly. "I'll see what else is in the bag."

There was a china poodle, a toilet brush, a thermos and a big value king-size box of soap powder.

"Be careful with the poo..." Nelly closed her eyes and winced as Slop lobbed the china poodle back into the darkness, smashing it against the wall.

"...dle," sighed Nelly.

"Oops!" said Slop.

Nelly watched dumbfounded as Slop sprouted more feelers than a sea anemone.

Nelly reached for bag number three.

"Cross your fingers," said Nelly.

"How many?" gurgled Slop.

"As many as you've got!" laughed Nelly.

"AHA!" whooped Nelly. "You can have all the arms and legs in the world but it won't help you beat me at Scrabble!" Slop slithered up close as Nelly pulled a Scrabble box out of the bag and laid the board out on the floor. She emptied the letters into one of the carrier bags and gave them a shake.

"Are these the instructions?" gurgled Slop, passing the lid of the box in front of three of his eyes.

"Yup," said Nelly. "Would you like me to read them to you?"

"I've just read them," gurgled Slop, reaching into the bag with a long sinuous feeler and drawing the letter J.

Nelly placed her hand in the bag, pulled out her letter and peered at it.

"E! E is lower than J so that means I go first!"

"OK," gurgled Slop, unphased by Nelly's early advantage.

Nelly took her first seven letters and arranged them on her rack. Slop plunged seven feelers into the bag and took out his letters too.

After much frowning and lip nibbling, Nelly placed her first word on the board.

"FARM ... that's eighteen points to me."

"Is it my turn now?" gurgled Slop.

"Yes," said Nelly, placing four new letters on her rack.

"Ninety-nine points for me," gurgled Slop, placing all seven of his letters down on the board.

Nelly placed her hands on her hips. "JABUK-OOG? What kind of a word is JABUKOOG?"

"It's Squurmese for "thank you," gurgled Slop, reaching into the bag for another seven letters.

"Oh," said Nelly, writing down Slop's score and then frowning intensely at her letters.

After three long minutes, her face broke into

a smile.

"JELLY!" she pronounced triumphantly. "Twenty-three points to me!"

"One hundred and twenty-two points to me," gurgled Slop, placing seven more letters down on the Scrabble board.

"GONZIBOX? What's GONZIBOX?" exclaimed Nelly.

"It's where Squurms keep their fish food," gurgled Slop, adding his score to the pad.

"I thought you said you fed your fish piranhas?"

"We do," gurgled Slop, "but we keep our piranhas in a gonzibox."

"Oh," said Nelly, sensing that her worst ever Scrabble defeat was approaching.

Slop was as good at Scrabble as he was at bat and ball. Nelly learnt that a QUAILFADY was a small furry monster with two trunks that only came out at night. She discovered that a SMOVGROT was a kind of woodlice jam, and that a WEENIPWOTCH was the hairy tuft between a Huffaluk's toes.

"I win!" gurgled Slop. "Nine hundred and fifty-seven points to one hundred and six."

"That's because you got all the best letters," huffed Nelly.

"I always win!" gurgled Slop. "What should we play now?"

Nelly puffed out her cheeks. She was all gamed out. She stood up with a sigh and flopped out on to the sofa. What could they play? What could they play? She looked around the room for inspiration. Nothing sprang from the white rubber wallpaper and she drew a blank from the white plastic floor too. The clock on the wall said 7:15. Dollop and Splat wouldn't be back for almost two hours.

"Let's play I Spy!" gurgled Slop. "I Spy with my six yellow eyes..."

"Let's not," said Nelly.

Slop placed the bootsale toys back into their bags and returned them to the cupboard under the stairs.

"I know what we can do!" said Nelly, springing off the sofa and turning in the direction of the kitchen.

"What?" gurgled Slop.

"PANCAKES!" said Nelly. "Do you like pancakes?"

"How do you play pancakes?" gurgled Slop.

"You don't play 'em, you eat 'em!" said Nelly. "Have you got any eggs?"

"There's loads in the fridge," gurgled Slop.

"Have you got any milk?"

"Next to the eggs," gurgled Slop.

"Then pancakes it is!" said Nelly.

6

Nelly marched into the Squurms's kitchen feeling quite pleased with herself. Despite Asti's best efforts to stop her enjoying pancakes at home, she could now enjoy some with Slop. Even better, with no Asti around Nelly could eat as many pancakes as she liked.

Her mom had taught her how to make them. They were really simple to cook.

"I'll need some flour too, Slop," said Nelly, scanning the shiny chrome doors of the Squurms's kitchen wall cabinets.

"I don't know what that is," gurgled Slop. "Try in there," he said, sprouting a feeler from his chest and spiralling it through the air in the direction of a cupboard door.

Nelly ran her fingertips over the smooth

surface of the cupboard door. Like the door under the stairs there were no handles.

Slop did the honors, opening the wall cabinet door with one sucker and the fridge door with another.

"That looks like flour," said Nelly, taking a silver packet of soft white powder off the shelf and giving it a sniff. She stuck her finger in and gave it a lick. It tasted sweeter than flour, but Nelly decided to give it a go.

"Eggs," gurgled Slop.

Nelly turned around and shuddered. Slop was juggling again.

"Careful, Slop, you might drop them!" she gasped.

Slop withdrew all fifteen feelers and let the eggs fall to the floor. They bounced off the floor tiles like super balls and returned to their box.

"What kind of eggs are they?" gasped Nelly.

"They're Veri eggs of course," gurgled Slop. "Haven't you seen a Veri egg before?"

Nelly began to feel foolish for not having seen

a Veri egg before and then reminded herself that of course she hadn't seen a Veri egg before! She'd never made a pancake for a Squurm before either!

"Let me see one," said Nelly inquisitively. Slop tossed a Veri egg to Nelly, who caught it in both hands and then cupped it in her palms. It felt about as heavy as an ordinary chicken egg, and if anything, looked slightly whiter.

"What is a Veri?" asked Nelly suspiciously.

"It's a bird of course!" gurgled Slop. "It's got three beaks – two at the front of its head, one at the back – and four wings covered in leathers."

"Don't you mean feathers?"

"No, Grimps have feathers, Veris have leathers. They're kind of leathery feathers. Mom says they're ever so difficult to pluck."

Nelly nodded blankly and then took a closer look at the egg in her palms.

"How do you crack them open?"

"You don't crack them, you unscrew them," gurgled Slop, placing two feelers top and bottom of an egg and twisting it in opposite directions.

Nelly watched enthralled as the Veri egg shell parted cleanly to reveal a glistening green yolk inside, about the size of a ping-pong ball. Slop held it under her nose. It smelt just like marzipan. These were going to be *very* different pancakes!

"All we need now is milk, a mixing bowl and a frying pan!" said Nelly. Slop duly obliged, producing all three at once from three different directions.

Nelly looked at the milk. It was blue. It smelt fresh enough, but it was the color of an Easter egg. She wasn't at all sure she wanted to know from which creature it had been milked and so instead of asking any further questions she simply poured.

Into the mixing bowl it went. Along with the yolks of four Veri eggs and the flour from the silver packet. The mixture went stiff almost instantly.

"More milk!" cried Nelly.

Into the mixing bowl it went. Along with the yolks of four Veri eggs.

"Coming up," gurgled Slop.

"More milk again!" cried Nelly. Her arms were already beginning to ache.

"Coming up again!" gurgled Slop. "Do you want me to whisk?"

Nelly puffed out her cheeks and looked at Slop. The advantage of having twenty arms to whisk with was easy to figure. She handed Slop the bowl with a grateful sigh and carried the frying pan to the stove. It was an electric stove, not very different from the one her mom used at home.

"Butter," said Nelly under her breath. "I need to melt a knob of..."

A packet of butter was hovering before her eyes. She reached up and took it from the feeler that was dangling above her head.

"Thank you, Slop," she said, opening the packet.

"My pleasure," gurgled Slop.

The butter was yellow. With black zebra stripes. Nelly smiled adventurously and broke two large chunks into the pan. It sizzled like butter and browned like butter, but the stripes crisped like bacon before dissolving into ash.

"Are you ready with the mixture, Slop?"

Slop gave the mixture a quick whisk with his feelers and then passed the bowl to Nelly.

"Here goes," said Nelly, pouring in the first measure of pancake batter.

Slop stood back warily as the frying pan began to sizzle.

"Looking good!" said Nelly, paddling the mixture gently. "Smells delicious too!"

Slop's nostrils began to twitch as the kitchen filled with the aroma of almonds, peanut butter and strawberry sauce. Nelly lifted the gleaming silver frying pan off the stove ring and prepared to toss her first ever Squurm pancake.

"Now you have to be careful when you do this, Slop, or your pancake can end up stuck to the ceiling."

Slop looked up at the ceiling and then back at the frying pan.

"Here goes," said Nelly, taking the frying pan handle in both hands and getting ready to flip. With a sharp upward movement Nelly sent the pancake nowhere. It refused to budge. It wasn't stuck to the pan, in fact it was quite the lightest, fluffiest looking pancake that Nelly had ever seen. But flip it wouldn't.

"Maybe it's *floor* not flour," gurgled Slop.

Nelly tried again, lowering the frying pan and then hurling it upwards with all her might. But it was no use. She had made the world's first gravity-defying pancake.

"Oh well," smiled Nelly, placing the frying pan on the side. "We'll just have to eat it like it is."

Slop reached two plates down from a cupboard and took some knives and forks out of a drawer. Nelly slid the pancake onto a plate and cut it in half. The smell of strawberry sauce wafted stronger as the pancake divided.

"Half for you, Slop, and half for me!" smiled Nelly.

Slop's orange lava-like body rippled from top to bottom as the first forkful of pancake disappeared inside his lips. Nelly nodded her agreement, chewing slowly and deliberately, savouring every moment. The first pancake was delicious. So was the second pancake. In fact, so was the third and the fourth. There was no need for golden syrup or sugar or jam. They were quite sweet enough as they were. But after her sixth Nelly began to feel rather queasy.

"I think I've had enough pancakes now," said Nelly with a belch.

"Me too," gurgled Slop with a squelch. "What should we play now?"

"Oh Slop!" groaned Nelly. "Aren't you worn out yet?"

"How about hide and seek?" gurgled Slop.

Nelly looked at her watch. There was plenty of time for another game.

"All right Slop," sighed Nelly. "You win. Hide and seek it is."

7

"You hide first!" gurgled Slop, his glistening orange body rippling with excitement.

Nelly burped again and trotted queasily in the direction of the living room.

"What should I count to?" gurgled Slop. "A million? A zillion? A frillion?"

"A hundred will do!" laughed Nelly.

"Forwards or backwards?" gurgled Slop.

"Any way you like!" shouted Nelly, squeezing under the shredda tank and pressing herself as far back against the wall as she could go. "And make sure you close your eyes. All six of them!"

Slop paused at forty-three and a half, placed a sucker over each egg-yolky eye and then proceeded to count upwards to a hundred in fractions.

"Coming! Ready or not!" he gurgled. "I see you!" he gurgled again, sending a long sinuous feeler into the living room through the beaded curtain, under the shredda tank and tapping Nelly on the nose.

Nelly sighed and then wriggled out from her hiding place.

"How can you possibly see me when you're not even in the same room?" she protested.

"Your pulse gave you away!" gurgled Slop. "I win!"

Nelly stood up and put her hands on her hips. "You don't win. It just means it's your turn to hide and my turn to seek."

"Close your eyes and count to a hundred then!" gurgled Slop. "I'm going to hide now."

Nelly cupped her hands over her eyes and began to count. She kept her ears open for clues but heard nothing except the sound of her own voice.

"Ninety-eight, ninety-nine, a hundred! Coming! Ready or not!" she called.

The house fell silent.

Nelly turned in the direction of the curtain and slid her hands through the beads. They parted with a soft jangle as she made her way through into the living room.

Her eyes dropped to the floor beneath the green plastic curtains hanging on either side of the bay window. Slop wasn't hiding there.

"Too obvious," she murmured, skirting around the armchairs and then dropping to her knees to see if Slop had squeezed under the tiny gap beneath the sofa. He wasn't hiding there either.

She stood up and padded barefoot across the white rubber carpet tiles and pried open the door of the games cupboard. There was no sign of the little orange rascal in there either.

Nelly frowned and took ten determined strides into the kitchen. She squinted into the narrow gaps between the units and then pulled open the kitchen cupboards with a fork. The shelves were lined with groceries of the grossest kind, tins of squeek liver in bitter bean sauce, pickled jov cheeks, mungus steaks, boil in the bag lumpit and family packets of squash batter were piled high. But there was no sign of Slop.

Nelly scratched her head. She was beginning to sense that she had a challenge on her hands. Wherever Slop was hiding, you could be sure that he wasn't going to be easy to find. She opened the fridge door and lifted the flap of the freezer compartment. The space inside was already occupied. Not by Slop, but by a packet of frozen weeps.

Nelly closed the fridge and turned towards the trash can. She placed her foot on the red chromium pedal and pressed down. The lid flapped open to reveal the leftovers from the Squurms" dinner the night before; four fish eyes the size of cricket balls and a scattering of cactus peelings.

But no Slop.

Slop wasn't in the living room and he wasn't in the kitchen. So where was he?

"I'm going to find you Slop! If it's the last thing I do!" shouted Nelly.

She paused for a moment, half hoping that Slop might acknowledge her with a gurgle and give her a clue to where he was hiding. No such luck.

"Maybe he's sneaked upstairs," she thought. "I know, I'll check the cupboard under the stairs, and if he's not in there I'll look in the bedrooms."

Nelly left the kitchen and returned to the hallway. She passed the flats of her hands across the door of the cupboard under the stairs and then knocked on it loudly, twice.

"Slop, if you're hiding in there it's not fair because I can't open the door without suckers, so come out right now if you ARE in there!"

Nelly waited. And listened. And sighed.

"I'll try upstairs."

There were fifteen steps to climb. All of them felt strangely spongy underfoot. "They must use marshmallow instead of wood," thought Nelly, placing her bare toes onto the landing.

She stopped for a moment and flicked her eyes between three doors. Two were the color of mushy peas, the third was the color of oxtail soup.

As she stepped towards the third door it slid automatically to her left. Nelly stepped into the room and looked down at a gently sloping mustard-colored mosaic floor. In the middle of the floor was a huge brass plughole about the size of a dustbin lid. Around the green rubber walls, rows upon rows of jacuzzi jets were pointing at her from all levels and directions. It was a shower room with enough jet power to clean a fleet of tractors. Pink fluffy towels hung from a blue plastic towel rail to her left and a huge piece of soggy black soap lay glistening in one corner of the floor. There was no bath and there was no Slop.

Nelly scratched her chin and headed for the nearest bedroom. "I'm getting warmer Slop!" she called half hopefully.

The first of the mushy-pea colored doors slid

back and Nelly stepped tentatively into the room. Tins of colored eye shadow were scattered across the floor and a paint brush was propped up in front of a wall length mirror to her left. It was Splat and Dollop's bedroom. A photograph of Slop as a chrysalis hung in a gilt frame by the window and a large double bed lay propped up against the opposite wall. Not flat to the floor like a normal bed, but fixed vertically to the wall.

"Squurms must sleep standing up!" gasped Nelly.

Her inquisitive nature suddenly gave way to a slight pang of guilt. She wasn't at all sure that she should be snooping around Splat and Dollops" bedroom. After all, bedrooms were private in her own house and she saw no reason why they should be any different in a Squurm's home. Anyway, something told her Slop wouldn't be hiding in here. She scanned the room quickly and moved on.

As she approached the second green door it slid open to reveal Slop's bedroom.

"Are you in here Slop?"

"Are you in here Slop?" she called, placing her hands around the door frame and peeking inside. Sure enough, a smaller bed was fixed securely and vertically to the far wall. The décor was the same. White rubber floor tiles, yellow Plastic walls. There were little or no places to hide except for a small aluminium cupboard positioned directly below the bedroom window. Nelly crept into the room, crouched down and ran her fingers across the cupboard doors.

"Are you in there Slop?" she whispered.

To her relief, the doors slid open. But to her dismay, music began playing. The cupboard had a built-in automatic radio. And Slop was still missing.

Nelly began to feel uneasy. She sighed heavily and looked at her watch. It was twenty-five to nine. Splat and Dollop would be home soon and she still had her sneakers and socks to retrieve from the sandpit and the dishes to do!

Enough was enough. She had hunted high and low and Slop was nowhere to be found. Reluctantly, she would have to concede defeat again.

"He's probably squeezed up a tap or something," sighed Nelly. "Anything to win."

"All right Slop!" she cried. "You win again! Your mom and dad will be home soon. It's time to stop playing and start tidying! You can come out now!"

Nelly waited for a loud gurgle and the reappearance of a victorious Slop. But neither happened. She walked to the top of the stairs and cleared her throat.

"I SAID IT'S TIME TO STOP PLAYING NOW, SLOP! YOU CAN COME OUT NOW, WHEREVER YOU ARE!"

But Slop didn't come out. The house remained as eerily silent as ever.

Nelly frowned and walked barefoot down the stairs. Why wasn't Slop answering? Why hadn't he stopped hiding? Where could he be?

"The sandpit!" she gasped. "What if he's been sucked into the sandpit!" Nelly raced down the hallway, scooted through the living room, burst through the beaded curtains and charged out into the garden. She pelted to the edge of the sandpit and stared at the surface of the quicksand for signs of entry.

All was still.

She stared down at her toes. "I can't go in again, it's far too dangerous! Surely Slop wouldn't have hidden in here?"

A thought too terrifying to contemplate iced her veins.

"The shreddas! Maybe he's fallen into the shredda tank!"

She spun around hard and sprinted back into the house through the French doors.

With a desperate lunge, she pressed her face hard to the glass of the aquarium. The pack of shreddas flew out from behind the bricks and barked ferociously at the glass, just inches from her face. Nelly ignored them completely and scanned every milliliter of the aquarium for signs of chewed up Slop.

To her relief there were none to be seen.

"SLOP! WHERE ARE YOU? I'M NOT PLAY-

ING ANYMORE!" she hollered.

But still there was no reply.

This wasn't a game anymore. It had stopped being a game some time ago. This was no fun at all! Nelly had promised the Squurms that Slop would be in safe hands, but she had absolutely no idea where he was! She double checked the kitchen, the living room, the hallway and the rooms upstairs. She even went up into the attic. She called Slop's name from the front doorstep in both directions up and down Sweet Street. She knocked hard again on the cupboard under the stairs, she even looked up her own sleeves. But there was no sign of him anywhere.

"What am I going to do?" she groaned. "Splat and Dollop will be home in ten minutes and I haven't just lost my sneakers and socks, I've lost their son!"

"SLOP! WHERE ARE YOUUUUUUU!" she cried.

But there was no reply.

Nelly squished down on to the sofa and racked her brains. She had looked absolutely everywhere she could think of. There was no time to ring any of her monster friends for help either. It was eight minutes and counting before Dollop and Splat would return. She was on her own, in every sense of the word.

She stood up dejectedly and tidied up a few games that were still scattered across the living room floor. With a puff of her cheeks she trudged barefoot into the kitchen and began stacking the pancake plates beside the sink.

"What am I going to say to Dollop and Splat?" she whimpered, placing the plug into its hole and turning the taps. "They're going to go bananas."

One by one she placed the plates, mixing bowl and frying pan into the water.

She took off her watch, glanced at the minute hand, and reached for the Furry Liquid. With a dejected squirt and a swish of her hand she began cleaning the dishes with a scourer. She was in a daze. How could she possibly have lost Slop?

The front door of the house had been closed and she'd only shut her eyes for the count of one hundred.

With a dispirited sigh, Nelly reached for the tea towel and began drying. She stacked the plates neatly to one side and then glanced again at her watch. Only three minutes and counting.

She dried the mixing bowl and then inspected it for traces of pancake mix. Satisfied that it was clean she returned it to the cupboard. Two minutes and counting.

With a blink and a sniff, Nelly picked up the frying pan and began wiping it dry with the cloth. She buffed the chromium base of the pan to a brilliant sparkle and then held it out for a final inspection. She tilted it first one way and then the other, and then back the original way.

She stared at the base of the pan and frowned. There was a reflection there that she couldn't quite account for. It was orange, it had yellow blobs in it and the black smiling shape of a mouth. Nelly's eyes sprang upwards. There, directly above her head was Slop, clinging like a pancake to the ceiling!

"I win, Nelly!" he gurgled, dropping to the kitchen floor with a squelch. "It was you that gave me the idea to hide up here. You never found me did you Nelly!"

Nelly didn't know whether to hug him or bonk him him with the frying pan.

"Slop, I've been looking for you everywhere!"

"I know!" gurgled Slop excitedly. "I've been watching you!"

The sound of a toilet flushing drew Nelly's attention to the front door. Dollop and Splat had returned. Nelly looked at her feet and began hopping up and down.

"I can't answer the door without sneakers and socks on," she gasped.

"I'll get them for you!" gurgled Slop, slithering out of the kitchen and into the garden.

In the blink of six eyes, Slop returned from the depths of the quicksand with Nelly's sneakers and socks.

She quickly slipped them on and bounced down the hallway to open the door. Splat and Dollop slithered in carrying a king-size bucket of toffee popcorn.

"We bought this for you, Nelly. We hope you like it!" Splat gurgled.

"Jabukoog!" said Nelly. "Jabukoog very much!"

Splat looked at Dollop in complete puzzlement. "I'm sorry Nelly, what did you say?" gurgled Splat.

"I said Jabukoog," said Nelly. "Jabukoog is Squurmese for thank you, isn't it?"

"There's no such word, Nelly!" chuckled Dollop. "You haven't been playing Scrabble with Slop have you?"

"Among other things," said Nelly, turning to Slop with a glare.

Slop gurgled sweetly and smiled at his mom and dad. "We've had a great time! We've played tons of games! Nelly's awesome at losing!"

"We've had a wonderful time too, thanks to you Nelly," gurgled Dollop. "We had the whole theater to ourselves! Everyone got up and left just as we walked in!"

Nelly smiled, crouched down and tied her shoelaces. She was exhausted. One thing she wouldn't be doing when she got home was playing games. She wasn't even sure she'd have the energy to fill in her secret notebook when she got home!

"I'll be going then!" smiled Nelly, offering Dollop and Splat a goodbye handshake.

Her offer was declined in favor of a cold wet squonk on the cheek from Dollop and a double squonk on the nose from Slop.

"Come and play again won't you Nelly!" gurgled Slop from the doorstep as Nelly undid the latch on the front gate.

"ZIBBLFLUDGE," said Nelly, with a nod and a wink.

Slop scratched his head with four feelers and looked up at his parents. Nelly closed the gate behind her and then smiled as the long, extended feeler that she had been expecting spiralled down the path and tapped her on the shoulder. It belonged, of course, to Slop.

"What does ZIBBLFLUDGE mean?" he gurgled.

"It's Nellyese for NEXT TIME I WIN!" laughed Nelly.

1

Nelly had had a phone call from the Water Greeps.

"How exciting," she gushed. "I've never monster sat on a canal boat before!"

"You'd better take some fish food to feed their children with," laughed her dad.

"No – a box of maggots!" sneered Asti.

"Or a pot of worms!" chuckled her mom.

Nelly sat back in her armchair and scowled in three directions at once.

"Sorry, Nelly," said her mom, "we were only joking."

"*I* wasn't," said Asti. "I meant every word. I bet maggots are precisely what Water Creeps eat."

"Greeps not *Creeps*," glared Nelly.

"Greeps shmeeps," said Asti. "They can call themselves what they want. They're all creeps to me."

Nelly flapped open her magazine and pretended not to listen.

"Asti, you shouldn't be so critical of people who aren't the same as you," said Nelly's dad, sensing that the jokes had gone far enough.

"They're not people, they're ugly hideous monsters," shrugged Asti, taking a hair brush from her hand bag.

"The world would be a very dull place if everyone looked the same wouldn't it, Yvonne?" continued Nelly's dad.

Mom nodded slowly, placing her hand inside a packet of asparagus and sea salt chips and focusing with a frown on the television.

"Look!" she cried, lowering a chip from her lips and dropping it back into the bag. "That's our bank! That's just around the corner, and ooh look look look, that's Coralie Powers from the school. She's being interviewed on TV!"

"Turn it up someone, I've got my fingers full of chips."

Dad turned to Nelly. She had her fingers full of magazine. Nelly turned to Asti. She had her fingers full of hair brush.

"Quick, quick!" said Mom. "Or we'll miss what's being said!"

Dad jumped up, jogged across the carpet and turned up the volume on the TV.

Coralie Powers was in breathless mid sentence.

"... they ran past me! There were three of

them. They had pistols! I thought oh my good giddy, they're going to take me hostage and hold me for ransom and demand millions of dollars for me, and demand a private jet to fly them to South America, and send out for pizzas, you know like they do in the movies, which is fine if you like pizzas but I'm allergic to tomato sauce you see."

The news reporter standing in the high street lowered his microphone, a little taken aback by the content of Mrs. Powers' eyewitness account, but then continued with a new line of questioning.

"Did you see their faces?" he quizzed her in earnest.

Mrs. Powers nodded enthusiastically.

"One of them had two big buck teeth at the front, big round cheeks and long grey dangly ears. The second had a big black shiny nose like a mouse, a big wide smile, big staring eyes and huge black circular ears and the third one had similar shaped eyes but a blue hat and a big orange beak like a duck."

The camera switched to the reporter for a well rehearsed look of concern.

"You said the robbers were carrying pistols. Did they threaten you in any way?"

Mrs. Powers shook her head. "No, they raced straight past me and sped off up the high street. But it doesn't end there, oh no! You might want to do a close-up for this bit," she whispered, beckoning the cameras forward.

"The strangest thing was that as they raced around that corner the first robber's head fell clean off!"

The reporter smiled weakly. "Do you think it's at all possible that the robbers could have been wearing masks?"

Mrs. Powers dropped her shopping bags to the pavement and wrung her hands. "That's it! Now that you mention it, they could *indeed* have been wearing masks! That would explain why the first one's head looked so wobbly! I thought he'd been to the pub!"

The reporter turned in the direction of Nelly

and her family and ended his report there and then.

"This is Jon Rippingale in Lowbridge reporting for YTV at the scene of this morning's high street bank robbery."

Nelly lowered her magazine and placed it on her lap. "It's about time something exciting happened in this town," she said.

"You're right for once," agreed Asti. "I wish I'd been there to see it. I wish they'd interviewed me – Natalie Dupre would have died of jealousy."

Nelly smiled, remembering the conversation she had had with Natalie about Asti's absence of brain. "How is Natalie? She hasn't been around for ages," asked Nelly innocently.

"We're not talking at the moment," said Asti, declining to go into details.

"I wonder how much money they got away with?" said Nelly's dad, returning everyone's thoughts to the bank robbers.

"A couple of million probably," said Asti.

"In cash," elaborated Nelly. "I don't think a bank in Lowbridge would have many gold bars to steal."

"I don't think they would have been able to race up the high street at all if they were carrying bags of gold bars," said Mom, adding her own bit of crime analysis to the conversation.

"Unless they work out. A lot of robbers work out – you need to be in good shape to rob a bank, I bet," said Asti.

"Well there's no chance that your dad was one of the robbers then," smiled Nelly's mom, casting a disapproving look at her husband's waistline.

Clifford breathed in sharply and decided to change the subject. "When are you monster sitting for the Water Greeps, Nelly?"

"Next Saturday afternoon," she smiled, standing up and allowing her magazine to tumble from her knees to the floor. "Can you give me a ride to the canal around noon next Saturday?"

"Sure," said her dad. "I should be able to extend my taxi service in that particular direction on that particular day at that particular time, unless of course I decide to join the local gym to particularly work on my new six-pack."

"That's a date then!" laughed Nelly. "Twelve o'clock next Saturday it is."

Nelly turned her thoughts to her secret notebook. She had decided to add the heading "Water Greeps," despite the fact that it would be a full week before she could fill in all the monster details. She threw a contemptuous glance at Asti and headed for the hallway.

"No you can't," she said, breezing past Asti's chair.

"No I can't what?" asked Asti.

"No you can't read my magazine," said Nelly.

"I've already read it!" smirked Asti.

2

Saturday arrived with a whimper and a rumble. The whimper came from Dad. He had decided to take up jogging that morning but had twisted his ankle turning out of the garden gate. To his acute embarrassment he had been forced to give up his new healthy lifestyle thirty seconds after taking it up.

The rumble came from the skies. Thunder was approaching and a storm was brewing. Nelly stared out of her bedroom window in the direction of the steep black cauliflower clouds that were banking up over the rooftops of the Montelimar Estate.

"It's going to be a wet one today," she muttered to herself, picking a thread of white cotton from the shoulder of her sardine sweatshirt. "A wet Water Greepy day!"

She pulled her raincoat from her wardrobe and skipped downstairs to the living room. There she found Asti sitting on the sofa draping a consoling arm around her dad's shoulder. He was slumped rather limply in his favorite armchair, dressed in an electric-blue tracksuit minus one sock and sneaker.

"Look out!" said Nelly's mom, bustling in from the kitchen carrying a light blue portable foot spa.

The warm water in the plastic dish slipped and slopped as she placed it on the carpet in front of her husband's outstretched foot.

"Stick your foot in there Clifford, while I plug it in," said Mom.

"Have you put the essential oils in?" winced Dad. "I'm going to need essential oils to recover from this one."

"I've put some fig syrup in," said Nelly's mom, "they're all the essential oils I've got at the moment."

Nelly and Asti watched with interest as their dad lowered his sports injury into the foot spa.

Mom, meanwhile, attached the plug to the wall. With a flick of the switch, the water around their dad's ankle began to stir slightly.

Mom turned the dial on the front of the foot spa two notches to the right.

"How's that?" she asked, as the water began to ripple.

"A little more," sighed Dad.

Mom turned the switch two more notches and the water began to bubble.

"That's better," sighed Dad.

"Are you still going to be able to give me a ride to the Water Greeps?" asked Nelly.

Nelly's dad's eyeballs rolled and his head flopped back into the cushions.

"Nelly, I won't be going anywhere with an injury as bad as this," he winced. "Unless it's a visit to the foot surgeon."

"But you promised!" groaned Nelly. "It's a two-mile hike to the canal and it's about to pour!"

Asti smiled at the prospect of a soggy sister and then sighed as her mom offered a solution.

"I'll drive you to the canal, Nelly. Make sure you're ready by five to twelve because I want to be back in time to watch 'Dancing with the Stars'. It starts at twelve-fifteen."

"I'm all ready to go," said Nelly. "I just need to put my raincoat on."

"Have you stuck the Water Greeps's telephone number on the hall mirror?" asked her dad.

"I'll leave you their cell number," said Nelly. "House boats don't have telephone lines!"

Nelly didn't know what the Water Greeps had. Ten heads? Webbed feet? Hairy knees? As she stepped out into the rain and ran for the car, there was only one thing she could be sure of. She was about to find out!

The car windshield wipers swished frantically to and fro as the rain battered and bounced the length and breadth of Sweet Street. Nelly looked back through the rear window in the direction of number 55. "I wonder what the Grerks are doing right now?" she thought. "I never did find out if Glug won first prize at the gog show."

The car forked right at the top of Sweet Street and splashed into Cracknell Way. Nelly's mom leant forward and wiped the windshield with her sleeve. The car was misting up.

"Where is the Water Greeps' houseboat, Nelly? Is it near the lock keeper's cottage or further down?"

Nelly shook her head. "IT'S FURTHER DOWN!" she replied, trying her best to be heard

above the sound of the car's defroster. Nelly's
mom turned the blowers down so that Nelly could
continue with her directions. "They said to follow
the canal road past the gas works and down to
the abandoned seed factory. Their houseboat is
moored up on the left just before the old cider
factory demolition site."

"HARDLY THE MOST SCENIC PART OF
THE RIVER ISN'T IT?" shouted Nelly's mom,
turning up the blowers again to try and clear the
resurgence of mist from her windshield.

"THEY SAID THEIR HOUSEBOAT IS VERY EASY TO SPOT BECAUSE IT'S THE ONLY HOUSEBOAT THERE!" hollered Nelly.

"I'M NOT SURPRISED!" shouted Nelly's mom. "IT MUST BE THE UGLIEST SPOT IN TOWN!"

"I'm sure they like it!" smiled Nelly.

Nelly and her mom drove on and ploughed through the puddles towards the Fudge Street roundabout. A family of Grimps lived at number 81 Fudge Street. Nelly had spent hours one evening trying without success to braid their children's feathers.

The sky darkened and then crackled magnesium-bright. Huge raindrops fell from the heavens and began to clatter across the roof like marbles. Nelly jumped as an almighty thunder clap suddenly shook the sky. "THANKS FOR THE RIDE, MOM, I WOULD HAVE GOTTEN SOAKED!" she shouted.

"YOU DESERVE TO GET SOAKED, MONSTER SITTING ON A DAY LIKE THIS!" her mom hollered.

Nelly's mom gripped the steering wheel and aqua-planed the car into Imperial Avenue. Nelly placed one hand inside the other and practiced her Water Greep hand shakes.

"If they've got webbed fingers I'll hold out a clenched fist," she decided. "If they've got no fingers I'll give them all high fives." She thought for a moment. "If they've got fins... if they've got fins... mmm, if they've got fins?... I'll just wave!"

Webbed fingers, no fingers and fins seemed to cover pretty much every aquatic possibility. Unless they were like hippos. No, that just couldn't be. If Water Greeps were like hippos, the canal boat would need to be an ocean liner to support them.

As the car turned sharply into Old Canal Road, Nelly and her mom began to shudder. It was cobbled all the way. The car began to vibrate as the tires juddered along past the lock keeper's cottage. The day boats tied up along the docks certainly were a sad and bedraggled sight.

The tidy clipped grass planted along the "Day Boats For Hire" stretch of the canal began to give way to longer, more neglected, straggly tufts of grass. Broken stems of brown twigs hung dripping in the rain and litter tangled with last year's weeds.

They were approaching the gas works. It was unclear to Nelly why they were called the gas works. Because as far as she knew there was no gas in them, and they certainly didn't work. In fact no one had worked there for years. The towering cylindrical buildings just stood there doing nothing except rusting, a cross between Stone Henge and a collection of giant upside down cake pans.

The car shuddered and juddered its soggy way across the cobbles past the gas works and towards the seed factory. The seed factory was a sad and depressing looking building with dark red brick walls, only barely held together by graffiti and crumbling mortar. Once upon a time, long before Nelly was born, the seed factory had bloomed. But now its grey slate roof swallowed the rain through holes the size of garage doors and its windows stared across the canal with shattered and empty eyes. Nelly would have liked to have scooped the entire building up in her arms and given it a big cuddle.

"There it is!" she cried, pointing further down the path to a small houseboat anchored beside the crunch and crumble of the cider factory demolition site.

"I can see it," said her mom, wiping her windshield again and peering through the hole.

Sure enough, just as the Water Greeps' directions had promised, a small houseboat was bobbing just directly opposite the demolition site.

"Pull up along here!" said Nelly, excitedly trying to get a better look.

Nelly's mom pulled the car off the cobbles and parked up in front of the padlocked entrance to the demolition site. There were no workmen in sight. The hard hats had been hung up for the weekend and the heavy machinery lay idle and dripping in the mud.

Nelly wiped a small spot in the condensation of the passenger mirror and checked her appearance. Nelly's mom turned off the engine and prepared to join her daughter in a frantic dash to the door of the houseboat.

"Come and meet your first monsters!" laughed Nelly.

"One two three GO!" they laughed, throwing open their car doors, tumbling out, slamming them shut and charging through the rain towards the high-glossed yellow bow of the boat.

"There's the way in!" cried Nelly, pointing to a heavily timbered door painted cherry red.

Nelly and her mom dashed to the edge of the canal and looked down over the side of the boat. Three steep, green glossed steps beckoned. Taking each other carefully by the hand they guided their toes over a thick tethering rope and stepped down. With a wobble and a teeter they negotiated steps two and three and then placed the soles of their shoes gingerly onto the deck. It was steadier underfoot than they had imagined it would be. In fact, quite astonishingly, it felt as firm on deck as it did on dock. There was another little surprise waiting for them too. It was a Water Greep, and it was standing in the entrance to the houseboat waiting to greet them.

4

Nelly stepped forward confidently and held out a clenched fist.

"Hello! I'm Nelly the Monster Sitter, pleased to meet you!"

A green frog-like claw extended from the doorway and a damp membrane-like webbing closed softly around her fist.

"I'm delighted to meet you, Nelly! Please do come in! Or would you rather stay outside and enjoy this beautiful spell of weather we're having at the moment?" replied the Water Greep in a shrill peeping voice.

Nelly and her mom blew raindrops from the end of their noses and laughed. "I'll just make sure you're going to be OK," whispered Nelly's mom out of the corner of her mouth, "and then I'll be off."

The Water Greeps

"I'm delighted to meet you, Nelly!"

"I'll be fine," whispered Nelly, withdrawing her fist from the Water Greep's cold, clammy palm. "He's lovely."

Nelly's idea of lovely was less than conventional: A black eely head, long, sinuous mottled green legs and a shimmering torso of glistening yellow fish scales which stopped at the waist and shoulders and had the odd look of a sleeveless disco dancer. It was hard to tell which sparkled most, the scales on the Water Greep's chest or the eye in the middle of its head. It was a single, solitary eye the size of a saucer. It had a jet black pupil in the center, ringed with red and white, and had a glistening, watery sheen. Nelly had seen an eye like that before somewhere. It was on the herring counter in the local supermarket.

"Do come inside and meet everyone," peeped the Water Greep, "the children are busting to meet you, Nelly."

"Would you mind if I popped in for a moment too, Mr. Greep?" said Nelly's mom, unable to suppress her desire to have a look inside.

"Be my guest," peeped the Greep, stepping to one side and welcoming them through the low cabin door with an extravagant sweep of its arm. "Come inside and meet my husband and children!"

"Oops," thought Nelly and her mom simultaneously. He was a she. Nelly's mom followed her inside the cabin.

"Watch your head!" peeped a chorus of excited voices from inside the boat. Nelly and her mom ducked beneath the yellow glossed frame of the door and looked up.

There, sitting politely on a bench of green plastic cushions to the right of a low-ceilinged cabin were three Water Greep children. To the left, standing small and proud was their Water Greep father. At first there was little to distinguish Dad from Mom, but as Nelly held out her fist to greet him, a red spiky crest rose from the top of his head and bristled like a perch fin.

Nelly smiled and her mom squirmed as the Water Greep extended both frog-like arms at once and closed his webbed fingers around theirs in a double clammy hand shake.

"It's an honor to meet you, Nelly. My name is Drip," he peeped, "this is my wife Drop, and these are our three children Plip, Plop and Seaview."

Five large shimmering herring eyes turned in the direction of Nelly's mom. "And you must be…"

"Mrs. Morton… Nelly's mom… call me Yvonne," said Nelly's mom a little flustered. After all, she'd never spoken to a monster before.

"There's a river called Yvonne!" peeped Seaview excitedly.

"No, there's a river called *Avon*," peeped Plop, the eldest of the three brothers.

Nelly's mom laughed. "What time do you need me to pick you up, Nelly?" she asked, quite reassured that Nelly would be very much at home with the Water Greeps.

"Is five o'clock OK?" Nelly asked, craning her

head slightly sideways to admire the crest of Drip's head fin in profile. It looked a bit like a punk's hairdo!

"Five o'clock would be splendid, Nelly," peeped Drip. "We've heard there's a boat jumble sale in the recreation park this afternoon. We've never been to one before, and we're very excited to go."

"You can never have too many anchors," explained Drop.

"I'm absolutely sure we'll be back by five," peeped Drip, "but we can return earlier if you'd rather."

Nelly smiled at Plip, Plop and Seaview. They wanted Nelly to monster sit for as long as possible. "Five is fine," Nelly reassured them. "I hope it stops raining or you'll be the only ones at the jumble sale!"

"I'll give you a ride if you like!" said Nelly's mom, who by now had lost all interest in her favorite afternoon TV show. "I'll be driving home that direction anyway, so I won't be going out of my way," she fibbed.

"How very kind," peeped Drip. "We'll be ready in two bristles of a notter's whisker."

"I'll be waiting in the car outside," said Nelly's mom, casting one final inquisitive glance around the Water Greeps's living quarters and then blowing Nelly a kiss and placing it on to her cheek.

Nelly squeezed her mom's hand affectionately and then joined Plip, Plop and Seaview on the green plastic cushions. The three brothers giggled. They couldn't wait for their parents to go.

Drip and Drop disappeared though a navy blue door at the stern end of the boat.

"Do you get a lot of otters around here?" asked Nelly, quite keen to see one herself.

"*Notters,* not otters," peeped Plop.

Nelly looked up with interest. She had obviously misheard Drip earlier.

"They're like otters but they're *not* otters, that's why we call them notters," explained Plip.

Nelly nodded slowly and then stepped across the cabin to get a view of the canal. "You must tell me if you see one," she said.

"Will do!" peeped Seaview.

Drip and Drop emerged from the low blue door and climbed two steps up to cabin level. "We're ready!" they peeped.

"Be good for Nelly, won't you children," they continued. "If you're not, Nelly won't want to come and monster sit again."

Plip, Plop and Seaview nodded in unison. "We promise," they peeped obediently.

Nelly waved goodbye to Drip and Drop as they left the cabin and then watched through the rain-drizzled glass of a porthole window as they frog hopped off the boat and over to the car.

Nelly's mom was waiting for them, getting wetter than ever. She tottered across the cobbles in her heels, opened and closed the rear passenger doors in turn and then scuttled back to the driver's seat. With the clunk of the driver's door, a rev of the engine and a frenzied wickerwackerwickerwacker of wiper blades they drove away.

"What should we do, shipmates?" laughed Nelly.

"You're the captain!" peeped Plop.

5

Nelly eased back into the cushions and placed her arms around Seaview and Plip. "Well, we might be a little restricted as to what we can do," she said, running her eyes from one end of the small cabin to the other. "It's way too wet for me to play outside, even with my raincoat on; and if you don't mind me saying, inside here it's a little..." She paused, anxious not to say the wrong thing.

"A little what?" peeped Plop.

"A little er... little," explained Nelly. "A little cramped," she expanded. "If you don't mind me saying."

The three brothers laughed. "There's tons more space downstairs, Nelly. Come and see!"

Seaview grabbed Nelly by the hand and pulled her through the low-beamed cabin towards the door that Drip and Drop had just emerged from. Nelly ducked her head and stepped gingerly through the doorway into pitch darkness.

"Where are we going?" she whispered, as the steps beneath her feet began to turn like a spiral staircase, leading her down, down and further down, beneath the hull of the boat.

"You'll see!" peeped Plip excitedly.

Nelly couldn't see at all. She steadied herself on the walls with the flats of her hands and then blinked hard as the light suddenly returned.

She rubbed her eyes and then opened her mouth wide. The Water Greeps didn't live in the houseboat at all. They lived below it, in an underwater penthouse built entirely out of glass!

"It's *amazing*!" gasped Nelly, turning her head slowly in all directions.

The room she was standing in was like an underwater conservatory, posh enough to feature in any home magazine. It was lit with flickering oil lamps that had the unmistakable aroma of sardines. Sculpted glass furniture was tastefully displayed across a polished aqua blue glass floor. Above her head was a sculpted glass ceiling and in front of her stretched a wide glass wall. The wall was as wide as two movie screens and curved around the boat in the shape of the letter D. At either end it was fixed securely to the brickwork of the canal wall with enormous glass bolts.

The ceiling swept low and was molded around the hull and glued watertight to the timbers with ship's tar. There were no drips or leaks or puddles to worry about. Every piece of glass was sealed as tightly as a clam shell.

"That's our garden," piped Plip, pointing through the glass wall. Nelly peered through the crystal clear glass into the soupier depths of the canal. She had a widescreen aquarium view of the canal bed in both directions.

"It's where we play," piped Seaview. "Mom and Dad aren't big on us playing indoors because sometimes we break things."

"*You* break things, Seaview. Plip and I don't!"

piped Plop.

Seaview blushed and looked sideways at a lava lamp, sitting on a glass display cabinet to the far right of the curved wall. Inside the lamp a lumpen clump of frogspawn sat motionless at the bottom.

"The frogspawn used to float up and down in funny wobbly blobs," piped Seaview.

"Until Seaview knocked it over," explained Plop.

Nelly nodded, but she wasn't really listening. Her eye had been drawn to the other end of the room, to a highly polished tangle of iron and brass.

"Mom and Dad collect anchors," explained Plip. "I don't know why. Anchors are pretty boring if you ask me."

"And me," nodded Nelly.

"And us," nodded his two brothers.

Nelly nodded again, but more to her self. "A giant underwater room? Sealed with ships' tar? Huge glass bolts? Plus the extra weight of an anchor collection? No wonder the Water Greep's home feels so rock steady underfoot! This house boat isn't going anywhere!"

"Look it's Mepps!" piped Seaview. "He's come to play! Is it OK if we go out to play with Mepps, Nelly?"

Nelly's eyes floated upwards from the anchors and then stuck like snails to the glass wall. A monstrous pike with a shiny red fishing lure dangling from its upper jaw was peering back at them through the glass. It had yellow and black eyes and a long mottled green body that tapered powerfully downwards to a strangely waggy tail.

"He wants to play fetch!" piped Seaview affectionately. "Can we go and play fetch with Mepps?"

Mepps wagged his tail again and then, with an extraordinary flip, did a kayak roll over on to his back and played dead.

"He does all kinds of tricks!" laughed Plip.

"He's huge. He's enormous!" gasped Nelly. "He must be over twenty pounds!"

"He is!" laughed Plop. "He's the canal record.

But he's never been caught."

"He never will be either," peeped Plip. "If any-one hooks him, we just cut the line."

Mepps sprang to life again and began tail walk-ing excitedly in front of the window.

"He's not going to have you for lunch is he?" asked Nelly, a little unsure whether to let the brothers play outside or not.

"Of course he isn't!" laughed Plip, Plop and Seav-iew. "Mepps wouldn't hurt us for the world!"

"OK then. If you're sure," nodded Nelly. "But don't go too far away from the houseboat. Stay where I can keep an eye on you. And if you have any problems, tap on the glass."

"We will!" promised the Water Greep brothers, hopping excitedly up the spiral staircase.

"Oh great!" thought Nelly. "I sounded just like my mom then!"

She took off her raincoat, lifted up a glass armchair and placed it directly opposite the glass window. She was just adjusting the left front leg slightly to the right when the water in front of the window exploded into bubbles.

Plop, Plip and Seaview had jumped into the canal from the top deck above and were waving at her through the glass.

6

Nelly could see everything through the thick glass but hear nothing. She waved back at them like a mime artist and then settled back in the glass chair to enjoy the fun and games. Not to mention the view.

Despite the murky brown appearance of the canal from the towpath, the water below the surface wasn't that unclear. It was a bit like looking into a cup of weak tea. In fact, in a matter of mere moments Nelly's vision had adjusted quite well.

The bed of the canal was blanketed with brown silt and looked a bit like a soft lunar landscape. Here and there strange lumps and bumps jutted up from the bottom, revealing the whereabouts of litter and junk that had been tossed into the water over the years. There was the buckled shape of a stroller wheel, the wonky spout of a watering can and over to the far left, close to the canal wall opposite, a discarded shopping cart.

There was a brass bed knob too. Not concealed beneath the silt but torpedoing through the water leaving a fizz of small bubbles behind it. It had been thrown by Plop and was being hotly pursued by Mepps.

Nelly watched in amusement as the bed knob crunched into the silkweed hanging from the submerged brickwork on the opposite canal wall. "Ouch," she winced, as Mepps's nose crunched headlong into the wall after it.

The bed knob plummeted to the base of the wall and landed softly, kicking up a cloudy puff of silt around it. The red fishing lure fluttered and then rattled as Mepps shook himself in a daze and then dived in hot pursuit. With a flick of his tail and a snap of his jaws the bed knob emerged from another puff of silt and was on its way back to Plop.

The three Water Greeps clapped silent applause through the window and prepared to send Mepps scuttling in a new direction. Two new directions actually, for as Plop unleashed the bed knob sixty feet bowwards, Plip hurled an old toilet flusher thirty feet sternwards.

Mepps lunged one way, and then the other before finally electing to retrieve the orange flusher first. With a thrash of his tail and a thrust of his fins he powered past Nelly and up the canal.

More silt erupted in the wake of Mepps' tail as he snapped up the flusher just inches from the canal bed. He turned triumphantly with the prize in his mouth and then set his sights on the bed knob that had landed some one hundred feet the other way.

Plip, Plop and Seaview clapped encouragingly again and beckoned Mepps back in their direction.

Mepps obliged for two of the fifty feet, but then suddenly slowed and dropped like a submarine to the bottom of the canal.

A school of silver bait fish were approaching, unaware that they were about to become dish of the day. Mepps concealed himself in the silt and allowed the fish to pass overhead. Then with a whisker fine flick of his pectoral fins he turned silently and followed in stealthy pursuit. It was game over.

Mepps disappeared out of sight up the canal and Nelly turned, only to find Plip, Plop and Seaview riding past the window! On three rusty bikes! She rubbed her eyes and leaned forward disbelievingly. But it was true. Their long frog-like legs were turning well-oiled rusty pedals and their webbed claws were steering corroded and broken handle bars in circular patterns through the silt. One by one, they removed their claws from the handle bars and waved with both hands through the glass.

Nelly raised her hand and waved back, open mouthed. Whatever would they be doing next? After six or seven turns and a brief but soundless discussion, the three Water Greeps turned in the direction of the opposite canal wall, kicked out with their legs and swam frog style over to the upturned shopping cart. As the rusty bicycles fell weightlessly back on to the canal bed, Plip and Plop heaved the trolley right side up and Seaview hopped into the grocery basket with another wave.

Nelly waved back and then squinted as a thick cloud of muddy brown silt mushroomed upwards from the trolley wheels. It was underwater Grand Prix Go-Kart time, Formula Three style, with one Water Greep up front and two Water Greeps doing the pushing.

The water muddied in an instant as the shopping trolley wheels skidded hard into the canal bed before speeding away past the window.

Nelly rubbed the glass with her sleeve and tried her best to keep track of their whereabouts as the clouds of silt began to build. But it was no use. Backwards and forwards the brothers sped, racing like maniacs in all directions. The more canal bed they covered the murkier the water became.

The Water Greeps

It was underwater Grand Prix time!

Sometimes she caught a glimpse of Plip up front, other times he was doing the pushing. Sometimes it was Plop's legs that paddled close by the window and on other occasions there was a playful wave from Seaview. But most of the time she could see almost nothing. The weak tea had turned to cocoa. There was nothing she could see and there was nothing she could do except wait patiently by the window for the silt to settle and the three little Water Greeps to reappear.

Nelly eased back into her glass armchair as the cocoa-colored canal water swirled and eddied before her. She wondered if it had stopped raining outside. It was impossible to tell from down here. She wondered if her mom had dropped Drip and Drop off at the boat sale OK, and if she'd ever made it back in time for 'Dancing with the Stars'. She wondered what would be for dinner that night and she wondered if there would be enough purple ink in her gel pen to write everything she needed to write about the Water Greeps in her secret notebook. She wondered whether Drip and Drop had an underwater window cleaner or whether they polished all the glass by themselves. And no wonder she wondered. The Water Greeps' home was awesome!

Nelly scratched her nose, peered over towards the anchor collection and then surveyed the rest of the room. There was a glass dining area located beneath the bow end of the hull and in the center of an oval glass table there appeared to be a glass fruit bowl full of green stalks.

Nelly stood up and walked over to the table for a closer inspection. The stalks had small circular green leaves. It was water cress. Or something very similar.

"*Not* my favorite nibbles," shuddered Nelly, glancing up at a glass shelf unit that was fixed just below the hull to the clean red bricks of the nearside path wall. The shelves were lined like a spice rack, but with larger, pickle sized jars.

There were no pickles of course. According to the spidery writing on the handwritten labels there was "Duckweed," "Lily Pad," "King Cup" "Yellow Flag," "Water Mint" and "Bulrush."

"Vegetarians!" thought Nelly. "Water Greeps are vegetarians. No wonder Mom liked them!"

She was just about to lift down the duckweed jar and give it a sniff when a sharp *tap tap* drew her attention back to the window.

The water in the canal had begun to clear and the outlines of Plip, Plop and Seaview were finally filtering through. It seemed the underwater shopping trolley Grand Prix had run its course and now they had turned their minds to something else. Each was hopping weightlessly from foot to foot outside the window and grinning from ear to ear. There was something else. Each had something in their hand that they were enthusiastically waving.

Nelly waved back at them with a smile and then stepped inquisitively towards the window. What exactly was it that they were waving?

Nelly took another step forward and her blood ran cold.

Pistols!

Nelly leapt towards the window and waved her hands madly.

Seaview tap tapped a bat on the glass again and waved excitedly back.

"NO!" shouted Nelly. "PUT THEM DOWN! DON'T PLAY WITH THOSE, THEY ARE DANGEROUS!"

Plip, Plop and Seaview watched innocently through the glass. They couldn't hear a word that

Nelly was saying. With hops and cheeky smiles, they raised the pistols above their heads and brandished them like three musketeers.

Nelly hopped up and down like a puppet.

"PUT THEM DOWN! PUT THEM DOWN!" she hollered at the very top of her voice. "YOU'LL HURT YOURSELVES!"

Plip, Plop and Seaview waved them playfully and began to hop like puppets too. They thought Nelly was playing some kind of copying game.

It was no use. Nelly had to do something and she had to do it FAST! She thrust her hand into the pocket of her jeans and pulled out her cell phone. Hurling it onto the polished glass floor, she spun like a tornado and raced back up the spiral stairs.

Plip, Plop and Seaview watched through the glass in amazement and then ducked into the bed of the canal as a jacuzzi of bubbles and green jeans depth charged over their heads. Nelly had jumped into the water too. She was five feet under. Her mouth was shut tight and her eyes were bulging.

She could make out the shapes of the three brothers beneath her, but she couldn't open her mouth to speak for fear of drowning. She stabbed her fingers wildly in the direction of the pistols and shook her head with gobstopper eyes.

Plip, Plop and Seaview looked at the pistols and then stared dumbly at each other. Whatever was Nelly trying to say? Nelly's lungs began to burst and her legs began to thrash. She couldn't stay underwater for very much longer.

She stabbed desperately again at the pistols and then redirected her stabbing fingers to the surface of the canal. A stream of bubbles began to seep from the corner of her mouth and her elbows began to flap. With a shake of her head and a kick of her feet she ballooned back up to the surface.

As her face broke the surface of the water, the air from inside her lungs whistled from her cheeks. With a splutter and a gasp she craned her head in all directions, hoping desperately that Plip, Plop and Seaview would appear.

One by one, the pistols periscoped above the surface of the canal, followed by the glistening herring eyes of the three brothers.

"What's up Nelly?" asked Plop, casually.

"WHAT'S UP!" spluttered Nelly, treading water as well as she could, fully clothed.

"I'LL TELL YOU WHAT'S UP!" she gasped, snatching the pistols from the brothers' claws. "DON'T YOU KNOW WHAT THESE ARE?"

The brothers shook their heads.

"THEY'RE PISTOLS!" gurgled Nelly. (The weight of them was causing her to sink again.)

Plip, Plop and Seaview swam forward blankly and lifted her shoulders out of the water. They had no idea what pistols were, and that they were *definitely* not toys.

"Help me out," spluttered Nelly, placing them awkwardly under one arm. The three Water Greep brothers paddled Nelly to the side of the boat and hoisted her back on to the deck. There she lay, like a bundle of soggy laundry plucked from a washing machine in mid cycle.

"Tell us what they are, Nelly," piped Plip.

"Let me get my breath back first," gasped Nelly. "And let me get this minnow out of my ear."

7

With the minnow removed, air back in her lungs and a circle of oil lamps placed around her for warmth, a relieved Nelly sank back into the polished glass chair by the window and prepared to lecture Plip, Plop and Seaview on the dangers of playing–or swimming–with pistols.

Nelly had first been careful to remove the three pistols to a position of maximom safety, high up on the shelf in place of the pickle jars.

As the Water Greeps dipped in, and began munching on water mint and bulrush heads, Nelly leant forward with a frown of deep concern.

"I'll tell you what these are," she cautioned, using her finger like an imaginary trigger. "It's a *click* at one end, and a *KERBOOOOOOOM!* at the other!"

A startled Plip, Plop and Seaview paused in mid munch as Nelly explained.

"Pistols are very dangerous weapons that grown-ups use to hunt rabbits and pigeons and pheasants," continued Nelly. "They are *NOT* toys. Gangsters use pistols, bank robbers use pistols..."

Nelly stopped in mid flow. "Bank robbers use pistols..." she murmured.

Her eyes flashed to the shelf and then back to the three brothers. "*Where* did you get them?" she asked. "*When* did you get them?"

"Seaview found them," peeped Plop, "at the bottom of the canal, didn't you, Seaview?"

"Last Saturday," nodded Seaview. "Last Saturday afternoon. They were in a sack under the water, at the bottom of the canal."

Nelly clapped her hands and turned Police Inspector on the spot.

"Let me think... let me think... The bank robbery was last Saturday... There were three robbers and they were all armed with pistols.

A week has gone by and the robbers haven't been caught and the pistols haven't been found... Until now! Seaview has found three of them hidden in a sack at the bottom of the canal. They must belong to the robbers! The robbers must have dropped them into the canal thinking they would never ever be found. But they have! Seaview has found three major clues!"

"SEAVIEW!" Nelly exclaimed. "Seaview... why are you called Seaview?" she faltered, momentarily sidetracked by a question she had been meaning to ask ever since she had been introduced.

"It was my idea," explained Plip proudly. "I saw the name on the side of another canal boat."

Nelly let the explanation sink in, shook her head and then returned immediately to a more significant line of questioning.

"Seaview, can you remember exactly where you found the pistols? And can you remember exactly where you put the sack?"

Seaview puffed out the yellow fish scales on his chest and nodded again. He was beginning to feel rather important.

"They were over there about 120 feet further down the dock, right in line with the center of the first gas works chimney. You can see the chimneys through the water."

"And the sack?" quizzed Nelly.

"I gave the sack to Mom and Dad," said Seaview.

"Excellent!" said Nelly, promoting herself from Inspector to Master Criminal Detective. "We'll need the sack for evidence."

Plip and Plop turned to Seaview and then looked awkwardly at their reflections in the glass floor.

"Dad uses the sack to polish the anchors," explained Plop, a little embarrassed.

Nelly frowned. It was the first setback of her criminal investigation. She stared at the anchors, peered at the shelf and then began scouring the floor.

"We need to call the police," she said, deciding

to call for back-up. "Where's my phone? I'm sure I threw it down here somewhere?"

Nelly had been smart enough not to jump into the canal with her phone in her pocket, but not smart enough to put it somewhere that was easy to find. Plip, Plop and Seaview joined Nelly on their claws and knees and began searching the floor.

"Found it!" piped Plop, crawling out from underneath the table and holding Nelly's cell phone above his head. The phone had skidded like an ice hockey puck a full twenty feet across the polished floor.

"Well done, Plop!" cried Nelly. "Let's hope I get service out here!"

They were in luck, and the police were on their way.

8

It had finally stopped raining. The clouds had parted and at last the sun was trying to peep out. Nelly
was peeping out too. Her face was pressed flat to
a porthole window in the cabin upstairs. She was
very excited. Everyone was. They'd never played
key roles in a criminal investigation before.

"Those are notters," piped Seaview, pointing
through a porthole further down.

Nelly craned her head right and then laughed.
"They're not notters, and they're not otters
either! They're rats!"

"We call them notters," piped Plip.

"We call them horrible smelly rats," laughed
Nelly, watching two long brown rat tails thread
between some building rubble in the demolition
site outside.

"And we call *those* police cars!" announced Nelly.

The police hadn't wasted any time. Sirens were fast approaching, their scream and wail changing to a high pitched yodel as the tires hit the cobbles on the dock. Nelly turned to Seaview excitedly. She could see one patrol car and a white forensic van too!

As the vehicles drew up alongside the canal boat, Nelly was already opening the cherry red door of the cabin and stepping out to greet them.

Two policemen climbed out of the patrol car and acknowledged Nelly with serious nods. One wore glasses and had a caterpillar thin moustache. The other was younger with ginger eyebrows that met in the middle. The forensic team took longer to emerge from their van. Apparently they were having trouble getting their fingers into their rubber gloves.

The moustache introduced himself first. "Sergeant Shrew!" he shouted. "May I come aboard?"

The Water Greeps

"Sergeant Shrew," he shouted.
"May I come aboard?"

"This way!" said Nelly, flapping the palms of her hands in the direction of the cabin. "Come and meet the Water Greeps!"

Both police officers strode purposefully across the towpath and stepped down onto the deck.

"Follow me!" said Nelly.

The two policemen ducked low beneath the frame of the door and stooped inside the houseboat.

They were greeted by the three Water Greep brothers.

"Hello Mister Policemen," they waved.

"This is Plip, Plop and Seaview!" said Nelly. "Seaview is the one that found the pistols!"

Seaview sat up tall and proud for a moment and nodded importantly.

"Can I take your full names please," said the constable, taking out his notebook and licking the point of his pencil.

"I'll give you mine if you give me yours," piped Seaview.

The ginger eyebrows arched above the note

pad and then turned in the direction of Sergeant Shrew.

Sergeant Shrew shrugged his shoulders and nodded.

"My name is PC Plum," said the constable.

"Paddlesump," piped Seaview. "Seaview Paddlesump."

"Plop Paddlesump," said Plop.

"Plip Paddlesump," said Plip.

"And I'm Petronella Morton," added Nelly. "Call me Nelly for short."

"And do you all live together on the houseboat?" asked the sergeant.

"No, I'm monster sitting for their mom and dad," explained Nelly. "They'll be back around five."

"And your address would be?" quizzed the sergeant.

"One hundred and nineteen Sweet Street," answered Nelly. "Over on the Montelimar Estate."

"I know Sweet Street very well," said the sergeant. "We were over there last Thursday evening, returning a stray bat to number 322."

The door of the cabin opened once again and the sergeant and constable were joined by the forensic team. One was a man and one was a woman, although it was kind of difficult to tell who was who. They were dressed from top to toe in white one-piece white suits that stretched like baby jumpers over their shoes and tucked tightly with a drawstring around their faces.

It was only the lipstick that gave the woman away. They had come armed with an impressive variety of portable equipment ranging from high tech widgets to state of the art digital gadgets.

"You need to dust for finger prints," said Nelly as they squeezed onto the long seat, in between the sergeant and constable.

Sergeant Shrew eased the congestion by standing up and pacing up and down carefully, trying not to bump his head.

"Kindly leave the orders to me, Miss Morton, I shall be conducting this investigation."

Nelly turned to Seaview and smiled.

"Is there a reward?" she asked excitedly.

The sergeant scanned the interior of the cabin and stroked his moustache. He liked the idea of living on a houseboat himself.

"There is a reward," he nodded slowly. "A reward of $50,000 has been offered for information leading to the capture, arrest and conviction of the three criminals.

"We already have three suspects under surveillance," said the sergeant, "but as yet no clues to nail them with."

"I'll get the pistols!" said Nelly.

"NO!" said the sergeant with a stern wag of his finger. "*You* won't get them, *I'll* get them," he insisted. "I don't want any of you youngsters touching dangerous evidence."

"But you don't know where they are," piped Seaview innocently. "How can you get them if you don't know where they are?"

The sergeant looked at the constable, the constable looked at the forensic team. Seaview had made an obvious but fair point.

"OK, you show us where the pistols are first and then my colleagues here will get them before proceeding with their painstaking forensic analysis."

"Good idea," said Nelly, leading the police team to the top of the spiral stairs.

"You'll need to test the sack for DNA too," said Nelly, tugging on the elbow of a white suit.

"I'll give the orders, thank you," coughed Sergeant Shrew.

Nelly led the police team below deck and over to the shelf where the pistols had been safely placed. In the meantime Plip, Plop and Seaview went looking for the sack. They found it screwed up and dripping with Flugwax over by the anchors. Drop had been busy polishing only that morning, and had every intention of continuing when he returned home from the boat jumble sale.

Seaview screwed up his face and raised the sack in the air. A smoking puddle of waxy green slime dribbled from each sodden corner.

Forensics looked at each other and shook

their heads. Whatever Flugwax was, it was caustic and strong, strong enough to wipe even the stubbornest clues clean away.

But all was far from lost. The sergeant's eyes lit up as he raised his chin to shelf level and spied the pistols that had been placed there. This was precisely the break his investigation needed! In fact, the pistols were such significant pieces of evidence, he could almost see the word "promotion" written over each one. All forensic had to do now was dust them for fingerprints, match them to the three suspects and the case would be in the bag.

The sergeant and constable stepped aside as the rubber-gloved fingers of the lipsticked forensic officer removed the pistols from the shelf for a closer inspection.

"Fakes," she said, after examining each pistol very closely. "Very convincing fakes, but fakes nevertheless."

"What does she mean?" whispered Seaview.

"She means they're not real pistols," said Nelly,

a little relieved.

"So they wouldn't have gone *Kerbbboooooom?*" asked Plop.

"No, thank goodness," said Nelly.

Real or not, the fake pistols were crucial evidence.

"You'll need to take our fingerprints too," said Nelly, "for elimination purposes."

Sergeant Shrew frowned. "I was just about to say that," he admitted.

"Me first!" piped Seaview, hopping onto a chair beside the table and offering three webbed fingers to the taller of the two forensic officers.

The male forensic officer looked uncertainly at Seaview's clammy digits and handed the portable finger printer to his colleague.

"I'll dust the evidence," he shuddered.

One by one, Nelly and the Water Greeps held out their fingers and watched excitedly as each was rolled in turn across a small digital pad.

"I thought you'd use ink pads!" said Nelly.

"This is a modern police force," said Sergeant

Shrew. "It takes cutting edge techniques to track down today's modern criminal minds."

"Our prints are very different from yours Nelly!" laughed Plop, whose spindly claws had produced something closer to a potato print than a fingerprint. A very slim potato at that; more like a French fry.

Nelly smiled and then watched with interest as the fake pistols were gently dusted with fine powder by the male forensic officer and then delicately brushed in turn.

"You need an infra-red scanner now," said Nelly.

"He knows he does," sighed the sergeant.

"That makes the fingerprints show up," said Nelly.

"I know it does," murmured the forensic duster.

The sergeant and constable crowded eagerly around the table as the forensic officer took a small fingerprint scanner the size of an iPod out of his pocket and passed it over the dusted pistols.

Plip, Plop and Seaview shielded their eyes as the purple light from the scanner passed along the lengths of the pistols.

Everyone held their breaths for a moment as the forensic officer raised the scanner studiously to his eyes. He passed the scanner to his colleague for confirmation. Her eyes darted to and fro for a moment, first to the pistols on the table then back to the scanner readings and then over to the French fry prints.

"Well?" said Nelly, unable to contain her excitement.

"Yes?" echoed the sergeant, unable to suppress his excitement *and* sensing an imminent promotion to Chief Inspector as well.

"There are only two sets of fingerprints here," said the male forensic officer, loosening the drawstring around his face and lowering his hood.

"One belongs to a Water Greep... The other belongs to Miss Morton."

Nelly turned to Plip, Plop and Seaview and pinched her face with a crumpled look of disappointment.

"You mean there are no bank robber fingerprints on any of the pistols at all?" she sighed.

"None at all," said the forensic officer.

"So Seaview won't be getting his reward?"

"Not at this rate," shrugged the constable.

"I knew there wouldn't be any fingerprints," peeped Seaview. "They were wearing gloves."

Everyone wheeled round and stared at Seaview.

"You mean you saw them?" gasped Nelly.

"Oh yes," nodded Seaview. "I was on the bottom of the canal bed by the docks when they dropped the sack in. They peered right into the water to make sure the sack had sunk to the bottom."

"And they didn't see you?" asked Nelly.

"Oh no," said Seaview. "But I saw them."

"And would you recognize them if you saw them again?" pressed Nelly, thrilled to be back on the bank robbers' trail.

"Oh yes," piped Seaview, puffing his chest out further than ever.

"Why on earth didn't you say you'd seen them before?" piped Plop.

"Nobody asked me," piped Seaview, deflating a little.

"Ahem!" said the constable.

"Yes AHEM!" barked the sergeant. "Do you think I might possibly be permitted to ask some questions myself? After all, may I remind you I am the senior officer in charge of this investigation."

"Go ahead," said Nelly.

"THANK YOU!" said the sergeant, motioning to the constable to reopen his notebook and re-lick the point of his pencil.

"Ask Seaview if he can take you back to the very spot where the robbers stood to look for footprints," said Nelly.

"I was just ABOUT TO!" thundered the sergeant.

"Ask him if he would be happy to look at some photographs of the suspects to see if he can give you a positive ID," piped Plop.

"I was JUST ABOUT TO DO THAT TOO!" roared the sergeant.

"Then ask him what he's going to buy with the reward money," piped Plip.

The sergeant's knuckles turned white and his face began to twitch with barely controlled frustration. With a squeak and a jibberjabber, he snatched the pad from the constable's hand, threw it on to the polished glass floor and began to jump up and down on it.

"I'd better take over," said the constable. "Now then, what was your first question?"

9

A trip along the docks proved fruitless. The rain had fallen so heavily that morning that any chance of finding the bank robbers' footprints had been completely washed away.

The forensic team probed and combed the footpath for almost an hour but there was nothing to see or find. The constable led Nelly and the Water Greeps back to the houseboat. There they found the sergeant standing sternly by the tethering rope with a black leather police file under his arm. He had managed to regain his composure and was ready to resume control of the enquiry.

"Ahem," he coughed, a little embarrassed by his earlier loss of command. "If you'd like to accompany me back on to the houseboat, Master

Paddlesump, I would be most obliged if you would cast your not inconsiderable eye over some of the images in my police file."

Seaview blinked at Nelly. He didn't have a clue what the sergeant was talking about.

"He wants you to look at some pictures in his photo album. To see if you can spot the three bank robbers."

"Oh OK!" piped Seaview, puffing his chest out again. "If they're there, I'll spot them for sure!"

Everyone felt encouraged. After all, Seaview had been quite insistent that he had had a very good look at the robbers and an eye as big as Seaview's must be worth that of twenty ordinary witnesses.

They returned to the conservatory beneath the hull and gathered around the glass table. Seaview was given the honor to sit at the head of the table where the heavy black police file awaited.

"Take your time," said Sergeant Shrew. "Turn each page slowly and look at each photo carefully. If you recognize any of the men in the book I want you to tap them twice on their left shoulder with your finger and say 'He's the one'".

"Can I look too?" asked Nelly.

"If you must," sighed the sergeant.

Nelly squeezed up alongside Seaview and peered inquisitively over his shoulder. Seaview reached forward with his spindly, froggy claw and opened the first page.

All eyes fell on Seaview's one eye. The black bullet pupil in the bullseye red center stared intently at the first photograph and then progressed steadily to the next and the next. Nelly was quite surprised by the rogues on display. None of the criminals looked like criminals at all! There were no scars or scowls or boxer flattened noses. Everyone looked quite normal. In fact if this was what criminals looked like then Nelly half supposed there was a chance of seeing her Science teacher in there.

Seaview turned the first page and suddenly looked up at the constable.

"It's my good for nothing cousin," explained the

constable, a little embarrassed to be related in any
way at all to a mug shot. The sergeant blushed,
Nelly giggled and Seaview returned to the book.

One by one, whisker by whisker, freckle by
freckle, dimple by dimple, Seaview studied every
feature of every face. Sometimes he paused long
and most times he stared hard, but each time he
moved on. Finally, with a sigh and a shake of his
head, he closed the book.

"It's no one in here," he said. "Sorry."

Nelly, Plip and Plop groaned with disappointment. They were sure Seaview would solve the
case, but instead they had reached a dead end.

No one was more disappointed than Sergeant
Shrew.

"No one? No one you say? Surely there must
be some mistake. Have another look," he said,
opening the book, pulling three passport-sized
mug shots out of the file and placing them on the
glass table with a tap of his finger. "Have another
really good look at *these three.*"

Seaview stared at the three photographs in

turn, and then shook his head. "Their hair color is right, in fact it's an exact match," he piped, "but the shape of their heads is all wrong. The bank robbers' heads were much more curvy than that. Their foreheads were much deeper, and their chins stuck right out to the left. Their eyes were much more over to the right too."

"They sound a right bunch of weirdos," said the constable, forgetting the company he was in.

"They didn't have masks on did they?" asked Nelly before the sergeant could.

"Definitely not," said Seaview, feeling quite deflated. "They definitely weren't wearing masks and it definitely wasn't them."

"Well that's that, then, isn't it?" said Sergeant Shrew, nodding to the constable to pack up his notebook. "Our trail has gone colder than a polar bear's bottom."

"Sorry," said Seaview.

"There's no need to be sorry," said the sergeant. "I wish every member of the community was as helpful to the police as you. You should think about joining the force yourself one day."

"I'd like that," piped Seaview.

Nelly left the table with a sigh and walked over to the window. She stared into the depths of the canal and racked her brains. She'd missed something. Everyone had missed something. They were far too close to catching the robbers for them to slip through their fingers now.

She looked at her watch. The dial had steamed up after the plunge she had taken earlier, but the hands were still moving freely. It was twenty to five. Her mom would be arriving soon to pick her up and Drip and Drop would be dropping back too.

She stared blankly at the silted lumps and bumps littering the canal bed and then peered upwards at the surface of the water. The surface of the water, the surface of the water...

"That's it!" she cried.

PC Plum jumped, dropping his note pad in the process, and then Sergeant Shrew somersaulted across the floor in a panic, fumbling hopelessly for his truncheon. "What's what?" he spluttered.

"I have to call my mom before she leaves!" said Nelly, plucking her cell phone from her pocket.

Everyone watched nonplussed as Nelly raised the phone to her ear.

"Mom, where are you?" she said. "I need you to go home! I need you to turn around and bring something to the houseboat... I know... but I NEEED you to... PLEAAAASE... the foot spa... bring the footspa to the house boat."

The sergeant looked at the constable. The Water Greeps looked at each other. No one knew what Nelly was up to. A foot spa? What could Nelly possibly want with a foot spa?

"You'll see!" said Nelly triumphantly. "Wait till Mom shows up and you'll see!"

10

Nelly's mom arrived from one direction in the red family van, just as Drip and Drop arrived from the other direction in a white taxi. There had never been so many cars parked on that particular stretch of the canal all at one time!

At the sight of the police car and the forensic van, all three parents dashed from their vehicles and rushed to the houseboat.

Nelly did the explaining.

"... and now I need the foot spa," she concluded. "You did go back for the foot spa didn't you, Mom?"

Nelly's mom nodded. "Your dad wasn't very happy, but it's in the back seat."

"OK. We need to fill it with water," said Nelly, taking full command of the investigation.

"Water is one thing we're not short of!" chuckled Plop, offering to fill the foot spa from the canal.

"Electricity is," said Plip, noticing the plug lead trailing across the dock as Nelly's mom lifted the foot spa from the car.

"Oh dear," said Nelly. "I forgot you didn't have electricity."

"Lock keeper's cottage!" piped Drip. "There's electricity there!"

"Let's go!" said Nelly, taking the foot spa from her mom, clasping it to her chest and racing up the canal path.

Drip, Drop, Plip, Plop, Seaview, Sergeant Shrew, Nelly's mom, PC Plum and the forensic team followed hard on her heels. They didn't know why they were following exactly, it just seemed like the right thing to do. Nelly seemed to be the *only* person around that had a clue what to do!

"What was the weather like on the day of the bank robbery?" shouted Nelly over her shoulder as she raced past the demolition site.

"I don't know," panted Sergeant Shrew, already out of breath. "PC Plum, what was the weather like the day of the robbery?"

"Er..." wheezed PC Plum, staggering past the seed factory. "I don't know either."

"And you call yourself a policeman!" panted Sergeant Shrew.

"It was a windy day!" shouted Nelly, heading towards the gasworks. "That's why one of the robber's masks looked so wobbly. It didn't fall off, it blew off in the wind!"

"It was a windy day!" wheezed Sergeant Shrew, relieved to see the day boat stretch of the canal approaching. "Write that in your notebook PC Plum! And next time be more observant!"

A large group of panting bodies crunched into the oak stained wooden panels of the lock keeper's door. Nelly's mom weezed and put her hands on her hips, the forensic team doubled over with their hands on their knees and the Water Greeps dropped down onto all fours.

Sergeant Shrew and PC Plum gasped and gulped for oxygen like fishes out of water as Nelly lifted the heavy brass knocker on the lock keeper's door and rapped hard.

The lock keeper opened the door and then sprang back in horror as a stampede of police uniforms, white coats, and sparkling yellow disco jumpsuits burst through the door.

"Police!" shouted Sergeant Shrew, thrusting his ID badge up the lock keeper's nose. "We need your your plug sockets!"

The crowd of bodies tumbled past the lock keeper and into his living room.

"There's one!" said Nelly, skidding across the carpet on her knees and wrenching the standard-lamp plug out of the wall.

"Water," she said, "will someone fill this foot spa with clean water from the tap?"

"Hot or cold?" asked PC Plum, taking the foot spa from Nelly's outstretched arms.

"Cold," said Nelly.

The lock keeper reeled into the living room in a daze and then led PC Plum through to the kitchen. With a squeak of the cold tap, the foot spa was filled and carefully carried back into the living room.

"Put it down here on the carpet please," said Nelly.

As PC Plum obliged, Nelly pushed the plug from the foot spa firmly into the socket on the wall.

Everyone, including the lock keeper, gathered around Nelly, and waited to see what she would do next.

Nelly knelt beside the foot spa and smiled like a TV detective.

"If it was a windy day then the surface of the canal wouldn't have been smooth. It would have been choppy."

"Write that down," whispered Sergeant Shrew to PC Plum.

Nelly eased backwards and pulled the three police mug shots from her jeans pocket.

"There would have been ripples on the surface of the water," she continued.

"And that too," whispered the sergeant.

"So when Seaview looked up at the robbers looking down, their faces could have appeared different, they could have been distorted by the ripples on the surface. Their foreheads could have looked deeper, their eyes could have been further over to the right and their chins could have been further over to the left. Their whole heads could have had a curvier shape altogether."

"I'm running out of paper," whispered PC Plum.

"I'm taking the next pad out of your wages," murmured Sergeant Shrew under his breath.

Nelly beckoned to Seaview. "Hold these photographs under the surface of the water Seaview, and then take another look."

"But they'll get wet!" protested Sergeant Shrew. "You can't wet police property!"

"If they get wet, you get your man... or men," countered Nelly.

Seaview puffed out his chest, squeezed through between his mom and dad and then knelt down on the carpet beside Nelly. Taking the first photograph between his two longest fingers, he leant forward and placed it face up in the clear water.

Nelly flicked the switch on the foot spa. The water began to stir slightly.

"How's that?" she asked.

"A little more," said Seaview.

Nelly turned the dial on the front of the foot spa two more notches to the right and the water began to ripple. The forehead under the water lengthened and the eyes and chin swerved in opposite directions.

"That's him!" shouted Seaview excitedly. "That's one of the men that I saw staring down into the canal!"

"Are you positive?" said Sergeant Shrew excitedly.

"Absolutely positive!" piped Seaview, placing another photograph into the foot spa.

"And that's HIM and that's the OTHER ONE!" he peeped. "I'm absolutely, definitely, positively certain that these are the three men who dropped the sack into the canal that day!"

Nelly clapped her hands. "We've caught all three robbers!"

PC Plum threw his pencil into the air and the sergeant began hopping happily around the floor like a two-legged frog.

"You should think about becoming a Water Greep!" laughed Seaview.

Nelly was carried back to the canal boat shoulder high.

"Who's that waiting for us?" she said, pointing down the path to the cars.

It was the taxi driver, standing with his arms folded beside the boat. In the pandemonium and excitement, Drip and Drop had run off down the dock without paying for their taxi journey. Not only had the meter been running all this time but the taxi driver's boot was full of anchors and he wasn't about to lift them out.

"Don't worry," smiled Nelly, "the reward money will pay for your cab fare!"

"And some new bikes!" piped Seaview.

It had been one of Nelly's best monster sitting adventures ever. She had made five new friends, solved a crime and been given a booklet by the lock keeper full of free summer day boat vouchers. Sergeant Shrew had invited her to a tour around the police station and PC Plum had promised that if she ever needed a prison cell to lock Asti in, he would see what he could do. Mom had met her first monsters, the mist had vanished from Nelly's watch, her clothes had dried out and during the celebrations afterwards she had even nibbled her first bulrush. (Not to be recommended!)

"Who are you monster sitting for next?" asked her mom, steering the van across the cobbles past the gas works.

"Who knows?" smiled Nelly. "There's more

monsters out there than I ever realized. I'll just have to wait for the phone to ring!"

Sir fartsalot

IS ON A QUEST
TO DEFEAT A VILLAIN MOST FOUL!

Look out for the Booger!
It could be right under your nose!

www.sirfartsalot.com

Sir Fartsalot hunts the booger

A NOVEL BY
KEVIN BOLGER

Are You a Believer in Fanciful Things?
In Pirates and Dragons and Creatures and Kings?

Then sit yourself down in a comfortable seat,
with maybe some cocoa and something to eat,
and I'll spin you the tale of Katrina Katrell,
a girl full of courage (and daring, as well!),
who down in the subway, under the ground,
saw something *fantastical* roaming around...

www.zorgamazoo.com